Russian Law

A Law Novel

Camille Taylor

Russian Law

Limitless Publishing, LLC
Kailua, HI 96734
www.limitlesspublishing.com

Formatting: Limitless Publishing

ISBN-13: 978-1-68058-327-4
ISBN-10: 1-68058-327-1

Dedication

For my friends Leonie and Michael,
thank you, always.

Prologue

May 2009,
SVR Headquarters,
Yasenevo, Moscow, Russian Federation

Nikolai Nagregor knew time was running out.

He had to find out how high this conspiracy went.

Who could he trust? Who could he tell?

Elena was at the top of the list. There wasn't anyone he trusted more. But he didn't want to put her in that position. He didn't want to put her in any more jeopardy than she was already in, if he could avoid it. Being his wife was hazardous enough without intentionally placing her in danger.

Cold eyes followed him wherever he went, watching. Waiting for him to screw up and make a mistake. To allow his attention to be diverted just long enough for them to strike. Whoever *they* were. Nowhere was safe, not even the hallways of the building he had pledged his life to. Not when traitors walked these very same corridors, plotting against the country they were supposed to love and protect to their very last breath.

Nikolai planned to bring every one of them to their knees. To make them pay dearly for their crimes.

But he was also a practical man and had taken precautions should things unexpectedly go to shit. But hoped to avoid that outcome at all costs, not just for him and his country but for his beautiful, sweet wife.

He couldn't bear the thought of leaving Elena, to not be with her and see her every day. He especially didn't want to leave her alone with his secret—his very dangerous secret. His unfortunate luck to stumble across the biggest plot of his career. One that had the potential to cause great harm and reached God only knew how high within his agency. But as a patriot, he wanted to make a difference in the world, and so despite the overwhelming fear and stress, he also felt somewhat appreciative. Now he only had to do something about it, which was easier said than done.

Nikolai adjusted the security pass on his navy blue suit jacket and collected the file folders he intended to work on later that night after dinner. His job was never really finished. Something always needed attending to, more so with his most current case. He locked his office door and moved down the hallway. The walls were a traditional off-white and the carpeted floors a bland beige. Sterile was the word that came to his mind as he passed through the first of several security check-points. His pass beeped as the LED light on the swipe machine turned a fluorescent green.

He nodded to the guard, easily concealing the gnawing stress and concern battling inside of him. How easily it would be to dump the knowledge inside his head into someone else's lap. He would certainly live a longer, healthier life if he could. But the realist inside him knew that without being able to trust a colleague or even a director completely, he would have to face this burden alone—at least until he knew more.

He shifted the folders in his hands and thought about the coming night. His polished black leather shoes soundless as he moved in efficient, long strides towards the exit. He knew Elena would not be pleased when she caught sight of the folders in his hands. It had been a long time since he had come home empty handed and he wished with all his heart tonight could've been one of those nights. The best he could do was try to beat Elena home and surprise her with one of his delicious home cooked dinners, then draw his hard-working and patient wife a magnificent bath surrounded by vanilla scented candles—her favorite.

Elena deserved so much better. She deserved a husband who always came home at six, but instead she'd gotten stuck with him. Elena knew the importance of his work. Hers was equally as important, so she cut him a fair amount of slack and he was grateful to her. He thanked God every day to be sharing a life with such an amazing woman.

He only hoped it would be a long and happy life. He played a dangerous game, one which could have deadly and disastrous consequences. Not only to him but to their country.

He often put his life on the line for his job, all part of working for the SVR—Sluzhba Vneshney Razvedki—Russia's Foreign Intelligence Service.

Nikolai swiped his access card once more, the security doors automatically sliding open, and walked towards the elevator that would descend to the ground floor. He would soon be home where he could finally relax, his muscles tense and his gut churning. He glanced at his watch. It was five-fifty. If everything went according to plan, he would still beat Elena home by an hour, just enough time for a quick shower and to cook his apologetic dinner. *Perfect*, he thought. He couldn't wait to see her face when she walked into their apartment.

Within minutes he was on the street, and an hour later he arrived home to the cozy little apartment he shared with Elena. The feminine décor she had assigned the room greeted him and he refrained from grimacing. He had allowed her free rein on decorating—a mistake in hindsight—where she could do whatever she wanted to every room in the place except for his study and this was what she had given him.

He had been shocked to say the least when he had first seen what Elena had done, but the décor was there to stay and while it wasn't the sleek, working professional design he had envisioned her giving the apartment, he hadn't bothered to voice his slight displeasure. Now, as much as it pained him to see it, everywhere he looked he saw his wife, his lovely Elena. That made it worth every Ruble.

He removed his overcoat and hung it in the small

closet by the door. He turned sharply when he sensed another person's presence. He knew instantly it wasn't Elena. He couldn't smell her sweet perfume that generally clung to everything it touched. His right hand closed around the pistol resting in the leather holster attached to his belt. All agents were required to carry for events such as this. He quickly withdrew the weapon, holding the Glock in his hand steady and ready to fire.

He crept forward into the main living quarters, keeping his breathing regulated, making no sound as he advanced on the intruder. His gaze shifted back and forth across the room as he silently moved, navigating around tables and chairs that stood in his way. He had home advantage. He caught sight of the dark figure. He was well hidden and had Nikolai not been a professional, would most likely not have seen him. He crouched down, keeping low to the ground as he approached.

"Nikolai, is that you?" the intruder asked into the darkness of the apartment. Nikolai stood still. He recognized the voice, had heard it often and smiled gratefully even as he let out a deep breath, relief pouring into him. He hadn't been expecting his visitor until tomorrow.

He straightened and returned his weapon to its place on his hip. "How did you know I was not Elena?"

The man started towards the sound of Nikolai's voice. "I can't smell gardenias," he replied simply.

Nikolai smiled again, thoughts of Elena once more filling his head. Making him yearn to hold her, even for a moment, if that was all he'd be allowed. Ever since he'd first met her in his office at SVR, as her supervisor, she had smelled deliciously of gardenias, her signature scent. She had been such a wide-eyed innocent back then and he had felt like the big bad wolf about to devour Little Red Riding Hood. He had been ruthless in his pursuit of her.

He cleared his mind of his wife. There would be plenty of time for that later when this matter was settled. Now was the time he could finally let loose what had been bothering him and get some input. The man before him had several years dealing with such problems. A man he trusted. He stepped forward.

Yes, everything will be all right now.

Between the two of them, they would sort out this mess, find the conspirators before they had a chance to commit their act of terrorism and potentially save hundreds of lives in the process. Nikolai's body relaxed, his shoulders aching as the weight lifted and he felt lighter than he had in days. He wasn't usually one to be so rattled by an impending attack but this one was no ordinary assault. He flicked the closest lamp on, illuminating them in a soft glow. He turned his back and reached into his desk drawer and retrieved a bottle of Stolichnaya—one of Russia's finest vodkas—and two small, sturdy glasses.

"I'm glad you're here," he admitted truthfully, without worrying about what the admission did to his ego. "This has been weighing heavily on me, gnawing away at me until my stomach is lined with nothing but ulcers."

His companion raised an eyebrow. "Then you haven't shared your concerns with Elena?"

Nikolai shook his head. "I didn't want to worry her."

He poured two fingers of vodka into both glasses.

"Yes, although it seems you've been doing enough worrying for the both of you. Are you sure she knows nothing? You know how Elena is and how attuned she is to your emotions," the man said, reasonably.

Nikolai held out the glass to his guest, who shook his head. Nikolai took a deep swallow of his, allowing the liquid to slide down his throat and warm his belly.

"No, she knows nothing. I made sure of it. Besides, in the past few weeks we've seen very little of each other. I've been working hard just trying to understand what I stumbled upon and then there was the time spent tracking you down."

The man shrugged. "They like to keep us busy and out of range. So you're absolutely sure Elena has no idea—"

"I already told you she doesn't. Why are you so interested?" Nikolai stopped when something in his overworked brain clicked and reviewed the past few sentences. His eyes widened, his movements too slow, so unexpected this turn of events.

I love you, Elena, skittered across his brain even as he drew his last breath. The man standing before him, the man who had called himself a friend, a trusted member of the intelligence community put a bullet right between his eyes, imbedding it in his brain. He was so quick, lightning fast. Nikolai hadn't seen it coming until it was too late, betrayed by the man he thought had come to help him.

Chapter 1

Six months later
Annandale, Virginia, USA

His cell phone beside the bed chirped incessantly. Lucas groaned and rolled over, away from the blond sleeping beside him, and snatched up the phone and growled into it.

"What?"

The voice on the other end sounded fully alert. "Gates, get your ass out of bed. We've got a DB."

His boss, CIA Special Agent in Charge, James Fitzgibbon, was never one to waste minutes. Lucas was already getting out of bed, stumbling for his clothes.

"Be right there."

He hung up without a goodbye. He knew his boss wouldn't be offended. Neither of them worried about useless things such as formalities and pleasantries when there was work to be done. Marlie sat up, clutching the blanket to her naked breasts, a frown burrowed deep in her forehead. Her brown eyes narrowed.

"Every goddamn night that phone rings," she complained.

"Yeah, the dead body is a real inconvenience," he said dryly, before looking over at her pouting face. "Sorry, honey, but it's my job. You'll get used it."

She obviously disagreed with him, shaking her head.

"No, I won't. Today when you come home, whenever that may be," she added sarcastically, "I won't be here. Not that you'd notice anyway."

Lucas groaned again. *Not one of those mornings,* he prayed silently. *Please, I'll be a good boy from now on, just please not one of those talks. I don't have the time to pacify her and I know I'll have to when I say something stupid and we both know I will if we have the talk.*

"Honey," he said as he stopped dressing and knelt on the bed beside her. "My job is very important." He steamrolled ahead when he saw her face grow darker. "Not that you're not important, but I need to do my job."

His job was important and he did it well. No, he did it *great*. So what if he had more reprimands than anyone else in his unit? He also had more arrests and case closures than anyone else. He admitted he'd become a little rough around the edges. He was colder than he'd like and preferred to work alone. He didn't take shit from anyone, especially criminals who thought the law didn't apply to them. He didn't believe in rights for the convicted or even the assumed guilty and he let his thoughts be known.

Usually loudly.

His boss, James Fitzgibbon, had recruited him when he was a D.C. cop and took him under his wing. Everything he knew he could credit to Jim even though some days his friend and mentor refused to admit he even knew Lucas. But he also knew that to get the job done right, sometimes you have to break a few rules, which was probably the only reason Lucas still had a job. Any other Special Agent in Charge would have booted him straight out of Langley.

Marlie shook her head again, crossing her arms under her breasts. She scowled at him, showing him her growing displeasure. They had only been going out for a little over two months but the woman had already tried every guilt trick known to man, starting with the usual—tears. Not one had the slightest effect on him whatsoever. He hated false emotion and particularly hated it when used as part of an arsenal.

"No, Lucas, I've had enough."

Strangely, he didn't care. He knew that was not an appropriate response when the woman you've been sleeping with says she's had enough. He knew he should be begging her to stay or making promises to cut back on work or some such shit a man ultimately did to keep a woman in his life. But Lucas just nodded, picked up the rest of his clothes, and headed to the bathroom. Hopefully she'd be gone by the time he got home tonight. Then he wouldn't have to deal with long goodbyes.

***

An hour later, several hand gestures and colorful remarks behind him, Lucas arrived at the crime scene in Chevy Chase. The house was the typical American dream complete with the customary white picket fence that immediately made him think of the Cleavers. He knew what he would find inside would be a world away from Ward and June.

He was dressed in a dark brown suit, his blond hair reaching his collar and he absently thought it was time for another cut. He pulled his badge and I.D. from his pocket, flashing the uniformed police officer on duty a glance at his Glock in the gun holster attached to his belt as his jacket opened.

The officer let him inside and directed him towards the action. Lucas's eyes found the body lying on the floor. Two shots to the chest and one to the head. Neat. Effective. Professional. Blood pooled around the corpse, the cream carpet soaking up the crimson liquid. He'd seen many scenes such as this over the years. Now, not even the smell got to him.

He moved around the body and gave a cursory look about the house. The Crime Scene Unit was in full swing, photographing the scene, collecting evidence while the medical examiner began his preparations for the body. He saw nothing which warranted his involvement and frowned. A plain clothed detective looked up from taking notes and caught sight of him. He started in Lucas's direction.

"Special Agent Gates?"

Lucas nodded. "What can the CIA do for you?"

The detective glanced at the badge Lucas had attached to his belt beside his gun before speaking.

"The DB, name of Igor Zimtov-tovski-strov," he stammered, having trouble pronouncing the surname, stumbling over the syllables. "The dude's Russian."

"So call ICE," Lucas offered, referring to Immigration and Customs Enforcement.

The detective shook his head. "No, I've got the right guy. We found this on his body."

He handed Lucas a small leather case, which he'd seen many times before; one was currently attached to his belt. He opened it, his heart sinking when he spotted the badge and identification. The man was in fact Russian and also worked for Russia's Foreign Intelligence Agency, SVR.

Shit, Lucas thought. It was really going to hit the fan and rain down on them. The Russians were not going to like this one little bit. They didn't take kindly to their citizens being murdered on foreign soil. He didn't like to think of the storm that would come down when it was known the victim also worked for the Russian Government. He wondered if anyone at the agency knew the Russian was in the country. Operating on foreign soil was not looked upon lightly especially by the United States. The thought didn't sit well with him. What the hell was Igor Zimtovich doing in Washington?

He rubbed a hand over his unshaven face. It was going to be one hell of a long day. Jim was likely to be in a foul mood and Lucas didn't blame him. The States' relations with Russia were sketchy at best. He only hoped they didn't feel the need to retaliate.

The last thing anyone wanted was another war.

"You better find the Russians some answers," he told the detective.

The Metro cop shook his head. "No, that's your job, Agent. We're just evidence collection. Everything we find is being sent directly to Langley. SAC Fitzgibbon's orders. Take it up with him."

"Shit." He ran his fingers through his hair. *Fucking fantastic*, he thought. He just loved dealing with the Russkies.

Chapter 2

Michael Ducane peered out the window of the Rossiya Airline's plane as it touched down at Moscow's Domodedovo Airport. The sky was grey and the cold air seeped into his bones. The landscape was dotted with white as the snow continued to fall. November wasn't usually the time of year a tourist planned a visit to Russia. He waited until most of the passengers disembarked before standing and making his way towards immigration.

He knew what he was looking for and spotted the man immediately, just as his benefactor had described. He handed his passport to the stout, dark-haired officer and waited while the man made the pretense of inspecting it for forgery, tilting it in the light to view the hologram imbedded. Not that it mattered. Even if the officer hadn't been paid to wave him through, the passport wouldn't raise any concerns. It wasn't his real identity and the fake was unlikely to be detected since it had cost top dollar and he'd used this particular identity previously without any issue.

"How long do you plan to stay?" the immigration officer asked in flawless English, his voice rough with his Russian accent.

"Two weeks."

The officer gave another glance at the passport before stamping it and handing it back to him.

"Enjoy your time in Moscow."

"Thank you. I plan to," he replied, before walking off to baggage claim and picking up his small suitcase. It was something he had done many times before. Every airport in the world looked and worked the same whether it was Dulles, Heathrow, or Kuwait International. Nothing ever changed and he figured he could navigate the busy airport with his eyes closed.

He moved confidently through the mob of tired passengers while his mind was on the job ahead. He ran through his to-do list. First and foremost was getting in contact with Alvin Pochenchov, his new benefactor's choice for providing him with the supplies he needed to complete his job. He didn't like working with third parties he didn't know but the money was good and he trusted his benefactor—in this matter at least. There wouldn't be many even in this God-forsaken country who had the balls to cross a man high up in government.

He didn't care who or what their agendas were. He was purely in it for the fame and fortune, not to mention the carnage and excitement that came along with it. He loved the fact his name was known to many, feared by more, and that he was being actively pursued by many government bodies, American and foreign, and had yet to be caught by either. He marveled at their stupidity. After all, he was just one man and enjoyed the game of cat and mouse, watching them chase their tails endlessly while he moved on to his next target.

He wasn't cut out for a nine-to-five job and certainly not a blue collar one, which was what had been waiting for him straight out of high school. People in the neighborhood he'd been raised in didn't go to college. Didn't amount to anything and died young and broke. He'd been determined not to follow in their footsteps.

His lucrative career had started one day when he was just a snot-nosed kid who'd packed too much gunpowder into a mailbox and watched it get blown to smithereens. Now, years later, he had perfected his cocktail for maximum effect and was *the* go-to man, his clients often outsourcing so they remained clean and off the radar. Many came to him for political reasons and feared the blowback or retaliation of such an act.

He wasn't concerned about taking responsibility. In fact, he left clues to his identity so he would be credited with the destruction and devastation. All it did was build his reputation and bring in more contracts every time the media showed one of his works of art, naming him as the perpetrator. There was nothing like free advertising, and what was the point of a spectacular explosion if no one was around to witness the beauty of it?

His next project would be the talk of the town and more televised than the Oscars. It would be remembered long after he was bone dust in the ground.

He exited the airport with no more delays and walked straight up to the dark Lincoln with blackened windows and climbed in the back. The car pulled slowly away from the curb and fell in with the traffic leaving the airport, heading for the heart of Moscow.

He had business to do.

Chapter 3

Special Agent in Charge James Fitzgibbon could feel the ulcer in his gut burning. He'd been on the phone with the Russian Government all morning, trying to mend ties and soothe ruffled feathers, ever the peace maker. This was one fucked up situation and it was only going to get worse. *What a way to start the goddamn morning*, he thought. He was supposed to have gone to see his doctor at ten and knew Maggie, his wife of almost thirty years, would be pissed when he arrived home and told her he'd had to postpone.

"This is your life, Jim," he could hear her saying, raring up for a premium nagging session. "That job of yours doesn't appreciate you. You need to start taking better care of yourself."

And she would be right, of course, like always. Not that he would ever tell her that. He took a deep breath, asked his gut to behave, opened the door to the conference room and almost stepped back when he heard the noise emanating from the room. *Jesus*, it was almost like a kindergarten class, all his men mouthing off to each other, laying bets on the most mundane and stupid things. He shook his head. He supposed he was a teacher in a way. His job was very similar—changing little boys into useful men, making them think for themselves. Which sometimes was a chore in itself.

The room suddenly went silent as he stepped through the door, giving him the honor he deserved. He was a legend in the field. They all knew it. They feared and worshipped him. A man they aspired to be. A man they could look up to and a man they could talk to.

He had been a part of the agency for over twenty years, had been on missions so classified he technically hadn't been anywhere close to where he had been. Missions that would have sent Maggie to an early grave had she known about them. He wasn't one for being diplomatic. He liked to cut through the bullshit and get right to the point. Although there were times diplomacy was needed and he had to work hard at it, subtlety and tact not part of his vocabulary. It had made getting his position within the agency difficult. But he was good at his job and the boys upstairs knew it. They also knew he had the respect and loyalty of all the top agents.

He gave a curt nod in the direction of the ten men sitting at the table which had been placed in the center of the room, dominating the space. They all looked up at him, eagerly awaiting their instructions.

"I've just been on the phone with the head of Russian Intelligence, Director Mishkin," he barked.

"Suffice to say he isn't pleased with the turn of events. Especially after what I had to tell him." He clicked a button on a small black remote he found on the table. The large screen on the wall at the back of the room flicked on and an image came into focus which had been taken several years ago. The picture showed a fit man of average height with brown hair and eyes.

"You all know this man," he said. "Michael Ducane's work is well known to this agency. His fingerprints were found at the scene in Chevy Chase early this morning."

Michael Ducane was a home grown terrorist with a notorious reputation who at last count had been responsible for more than twenty bombings around the globe, resulting in tens of thousands of victims from right here in the US to the United Kingdom and even in the Middle East. He had made the FBI and CIA's most wanted list when he was only in his twenties and they'd had a tough time pinning the bombings to him as he never stuck to one particular target. He had gone after cars and buildings alike, political and non-political targets, American and foreign. He was a man for hire. A man who could be bought by the highest bidder.

Fitzgibbon's gut burned. Not only did one of Russia's Intelligence agents have to be found murdered in his goddamned country but now Ducane had to be involved. It didn't bode well for either government. He knew the Russians were going to blame him personally for this mess and he couldn't fault them. He would be looking for blood too if it had been his agent.

He wondered what Ducane planned to do and who had hired him and for what reason. There were too many questions and not enough answers. They were shooting in the dark and he hated not knowing Ducane's agenda.

"We're operating under the assumption he met with the Russian national and likely obtained information from him," James continued. "Unfortunately we don't yet know what that may be. The Russians are being rather tight-lipped about their agent. It's believed they were unaware of his visit."

"So they say," an agent muttered loudly.

There were several murmurs of agreement across the room.

"It's believed Ducane has already arrived in Russia. From what I can gather, the Russian was privy to information that could prove lethal. Gates will be heading there shortly to head up the investigation." His gaze settled momentarily on the other nine agents in turn. "The rest of you I want working double time. Reach out to your contacts and let them know any intel gathered in regards to this is highly appreciated. So let's do what we do best and find the fucker before he has a chance to complete his assignment. Gates, a word?"

***

Lucas followed James out of the conference room and into his smaller office. It had a nice view of the parking lot. Jim lowered himself into his chair while Lucas remained standing. *This shouldn't take long*, he thought. Just the usual riot act before a mission. He should be on his way back to his house within the hour.

His boss sighed heavily and pinched the bridge of his nose. "I can't stress this enough, Gates. This is a delicate matter. A little diplomacy is needed. I don't want to burn our bridges with Russia, understand?"

Who would? Russia would be worse in any argument and could hold a grudge longer than any woman he knew. It was also the nation that had stockpiles of nuclear weapons left over from the Cold War. The last thing he wanted was a nuke shoved up his ass.

"Yes, sir."

"Watch your back," Fitzgibbon warned, fixing Lucas with a steely eye. "I don't like the fact the Russian worked for intelligence. The president will be attending a summit there shortly and I don't want him to find himself in the middle of World War Three."

"Relax, Jim, you've taught me well," Lucas said cockily, rocking back on his heels. But both knew he said nothing that wasn't true and couldn't be backed up by action. He had been taught well and knew how to handle himself in any situation.

James nodded. That was precisely why Fitzgibbon had chosen him for the mission. That and the fact his boss could trust him explicitly.

"Ducane isn't one for playing well with others," Lucas stated.

"Which is probably why the Russian is dead," Fitzgibbon added. "I bet he had expected to have a more active role in whatever the hell is going on."

Lucas grunted. "I just wish we had an idea what we're looking at. I don't like going in blind."

Fitzgibbon growled. "Well, whatever the target, I want you to find Ducane before he can fuck up our relations with Russia. Bring the shit home, Luc, and don't forget to play nice. I know you have it in you."

"Thanks for the vote of confidence," Lucas said dryly. "I'll tell you what, I'll try and be a good boy so long as my balls don't freeze and drop off, okay?"

Jim rolled his eyes and was probably wondering if it wasn't too late to get Austin to take Lucas's place. At least Austin knew when to hold his tongue and was a better team player.

"Sorry, Jim, I'm already on my way," he told his mentor and friend. He wanted the chance to bring down Ducane. The man had a lot to answer for. In Lucas's opinion you didn't turn your back on the greatest country and then strike out at it. As far as he was concerned, Ducane gave up all his rights the moment he became a terrorist. "I'll either be bringing him home in handcuffs or a body bag, but I'll be bringing him home," Lucas declared.

They both knew he was telling the truth. He'd never let Fitzgibbon down and knew it would be a cold day in hell if he ever did.

Michael Ducane was coming home—whether he wanted to or not.

Chapter 4

Michael Ducane walked across the Marriot's polished lobby floor, his companion Alvin Pochenchov striding beside him. He couldn't stand the man. He smelled like fish and his eyes were too close together. He made sure he watched himself around the Russian. Alvin was the type to stab you in the back or rat you out for a reduced sentence, whichever the case may be. His benefactor must have him by the shorthairs if he was directing him to deal with the low-life scum. He didn't like rats or men who were weak. But he was on a tight schedule and didn't have the time to be picky. If Pochenchov could get him his shopping list in the time required he could certainly put up with the man for a short period. Besides, he had come with a glowing recommendation and was well acquainted with Moscow's underworld.

"So you have everything I need?" he asked Pochenchov, eager to get the meeting over and the hell out of Moscow. He didn't want to risk being seen. He didn't mind the notoriety but he could do

25

without the heat. At least until his task was accomplished here. By now he was sure the body of the Russian traitor had been discovered and each government would be pulling out all the stops to avoid an international situation.

Alvin Pochenchov was, according to his benefactor, the best black market weapons dealer for miles which made him a high commodity. The man just gave him the creeps. His appearance was straight out of any B-grade movie, complete with a tacky leather jacket and gelled back dark hair.

Alvin spoke, his Russian accent thick. "Of course."

"When can you deliver?"

Alvin watched as a thin woman with large breasts sashayed past and gave her the attention she demanded before turning back to his companion.

"Whenever you want," he said, his voice husky as obvious lust coursed through his body.

The man was a pig. One who couldn't keep his head in the game. He despised men like that. He wasn't a monk. He could understand Alvin's weakness but just couldn't condone it. There was plenty of time for fun later but right now a lot rode on what Pochenchov could deliver and his life was attached to the fact that he would be able to hold up his end of the bargain. His benefactor wasn't a man anyone would willingly betray.

"As soon as possible," he said.

He was only going to get one chance at his target and if he failed, he doubted he would go quietly. He had a small time frame and wanted to spend as much time before the event making sure he had the measurements right. He was a perfectionist, after all.

Alvin stopped halfway across the lobby. "Very good. I will call you when I'm ready to deliver."

"Pleasure doing business with you, Alvin."

He reached out and took Alvin's sweaty hand in his and pumped it once before releasing, suppressing the urge to wipe his palm on his pants. Alvin was the type who thought everybody loved him and he wasn't about to burst his bubble. Let the deluded man think it was a pleasure for him when in reality it was a necessity. After the delivery he would never see the man again.

"I'm always here if you need anything else, Mike," Alvin said, propositioning him for future dealings.

He resisted the urge to strike the man down. *A bomb under his car would do nicely*, he thought. His brazen use of such an intimate name disgusted him. The rage inside him caused the vein in his temple to bulge. He decided to make a hasty getaway. He couldn't afford to kill the idiot before his shipment was delivered. With renewed interest he continued towards the hotel's exit, too busy thinking of ways to dispose of Alvin once he ceased being useful to notice the desk clerk watching him leave.

Chapter 5

Lucas opened the door to his Annandale home. Silence greeted him. The house was deserted. True to her word, Marlie had packed and left. Good. He'd never been a relationship kind of man anyway, never one for being home at five and having dinner at six. He lived for his job and only had sex in between. He had taken a slight chance with Marlie but like all his other relationships, it had fizzled and died. All his previous girlfriends thought they could change him. Make him something he was not. Not many women could deal with what he did for a living, the secrecy of never knowing exactly what he was doing and with whom not to mention the erratic hours.

He glanced about his house. Some might say it needed a woman's touch. He hadn't updated his furniture since college and the IKEA brand looked dated, not at all homey. Maybe one day soon he would hire someone to come in and redecorate. *Why not*, he thought. He had the money for it, never taking vacations. He lived to work but didn't work to live.

In his bedroom, he pulled out his carry-on from the closet and started packing. He came across some articles of clothing left by Marlie. He tossed them across the room towards the bin. He didn't plan on seeing the woman again and he wasn't about to go out of his way to return her clothes to her. As far as he was concerned, anything she left in her bid to get out of his life was fair game.

He turned his attention back to packing. It barely required much thought these days, the action second nature. He automatically collected his razor, comb, toothbrush, and toothpaste from the en suite. The only thing that ever changed was the locations. He had never been to Moscow before so this would be a new experience. He made sure he packed some long johns. It got cold in Russia. He was only half joking to Jim when he mentioned his balls might freeze and drop off.

He threw in his cell phone charger and zipped up the carry-on. He was ready. He tucked his passport into his pocket as he mentally ran through the GPS in his head, picking out the fastest route that would bypass the bulk of traffic at this time of day. In two hours he would be boarding his flight bound for Moscow.

Chapter 6

Elena Ivanova opened the large glass door and entered the building housing SVR headquarters. She swiped her identification through the reader and headed down the hallway. She had worked for SVR for over five years as an inter-agency liaison officer. It was a job she loved and did well. She had connections in almost every intelligence agency in the world. She stepped into the elevator and pressed the button that would take her to her floor.

She tried to drum up some enthusiasm for the day ahead. She usually wasn't one for counting days until the weekend but her work of late had left her extremely dissatisfied.

After her husband had died, she had been subjected to months of grief counseling and was made to see the agency's psychologist. None of which had helped her. Talking about the unfairness of life seemed pointless to her and the only thing that could make anything right other than Nikolai returning to her was closure, which she knew she would never get. Not while Nikolai's death had yet to be avenged. He was always on her mind and would never leave her. She wouldn't allow him to.

She sighed out loud when she entered her office and saw the stack of papers on her desk. The pile was never-ending. She dumped her purse into a drawer and removed her coat before sitting down at her wood desk. Her bottom barely hit the soft cushion of the seat when a brisk knock sounded at her door and was immediately opened. Surprised, Elena looked up at the man standing in her doorway. She stared at him coolly as he entered her office and closed the door firmly behind him.

SVR Director Vladimir Mishkin studied her as he walked toward her desk. She stood as he drew near. She knew how much he hated the fact that when she was standing they stood eye to eye. At five-foot-four, this was not much of an accomplishment on her behalf.

"To what do I owe this honor, Director Mishkin?" she asked, unable to keep the biting sarcasm from her tone. She couldn't forget how quickly he'd swept Nikolai's murder under the rug and how he'd punished her for not accepting his decision. She'd learned that day, months ago, who her friends were and just how little she could trust them and her colleagues. It wasn't something she'd wanted on the heels of Nikolai's death when she'd been alone and trying to understand why he'd been taken from her.

Mishkin surreptitiously glanced about her office, at the stack of paperwork on her desk before turning back to her.

"I need you to work on a case."

Elena's eyebrow rose. She crossed her arms beneath her breasts and leaned against her desk. She hadn't been expecting this. For the past six months she had been confined to her desk. Now she was being offered an active case *and* by the Director of SVR, the very man who'd benched her. Go figure. He must be desperate.

She nodded, understanding. "Meaning no one else wanted to do it?"

Vladimir narrowed his eyes. She knew she had hit the nail on the head. Rumors had floated around the proverbial water cooler that a CIA Agent was on his way here. She just never thought she would be the liaison officer. Nor did she particularly wish for the job. Americans had a rather bad reputation that couldn't be ignored. Rules and procedure that had been drilled into her meant nothing to them. She didn't understand that fly by night attitude. Her very existence relied upon rules and regulation, though her own husband had skirted the lines more than once. But it was a chance to be free of her desk and the duties that had her bound there. It was also the first step in reclaiming the life she'd lost.

"The American Agent is due in a matter of hours. I would not be asking you, but as you can see, I am in a bind."

"How long is he anticipated to stay? I have other work I wish to complete and don't want my time to be monopolized," she said sweetly.

"I would want your complete attention on this matter, Agent Ivanova. I don't wish him to be running about unattended." He studied her carefully. "If you agree to do this, I will reinstate you to permanent active status."

She smiled. "You must be desperate, Director. I've been told until I complete my stages of grieving and the psychologist signs off on my mental health, these walls are all I'll be seeing for a very long while."

She felt some satisfaction at seeing the Director mentally count to ten. She'd caused him more than one headache over the past few months but she'd never forgive his negligence in Nikolai's case and her reassignment. She wanted him to suffer as she'd suffered.

Mishkin frowned. "You're very stubborn."

"That's what Nikolai loved so much about me," she told him sadly. "But I will accept your terms, Director. I miss the people connection I once had, and let's face it, no one likes doing paperwork."

Mishkin studied her as if she was something under a microscope. She stood still under his gaze, determined not to show what lay beneath her exterior. "Are you sure you're ready for this? I could see if—"

"I've been ready for six months, Director Mishkin," Elena interrupted. "In fact, I've needed it."

She was sick of being treated like a delicate flower about to fall apart. Yes, Nikolai's death had devastated her, but she was stronger than they knew.

Vladimir nodded. "Very well, Elena," he said, using her first name, something he did rarely. "But step lightly. You will be watched closely."

"I'm not going to go off the deep end," she

promised firmly.

She had learned it was easiest to keep her mouth shut and work in silence. At least until she had the evidence she needed. She'd not be dismissed again because they believed her to be distraught over her husband's death. She was, she couldn't deny that, but her concerns had merit too and she would learn the truth.

"Then the case is all yours," Director Mishkin said and turned around, walking towards the door. Elena followed him out of her office.

"So, who is this American Agent?"

Chapter 7

Lucas hated to fly. He hated the cramped seats that didn't allow him to properly stretch his long legs out comfortably. He hated the damn in-flight meal and he hated the security checks at foreign airports. Not long ago, a multiple murderer and known terrorist flew into the country and had the welcome mat rolled out for him. But a hardworking solid citizen and CIA Special Agent had twenty questions thrown at him, his references verified, and had a pat down that came real close to second base—all while the head of security glowered at him.

Fucking fantastic. What a way to start the investigation.

Now he was in a taxi cab and after several attempts of trying to ask the driver if he spoke English was on his way to Yasenevo to the SVR headquarters. Lucas secured his winter coat more firmly around his body, the cold climate getting to him even through the layers of clothes he wore. It wasn't like Washington weather, a deep chill cut into his bones and refused to leave. He watched as the driver swerved through the traffic, shouting what Lucas guessed to be a profanity. His thick, hairy arm rose with a rude gesture to accompany his remark at a truck driver who cut him off as they drove past Moscow Automobile Ring Road.

Lucas stared out his window as snow drifted down to the road, adding to the already heavy layer. He guessed by midnight there would be several inches on the ground and Moscowians tomorrow would be battling their way through the sludge. He never understood how people could believe snow to be so beautiful. Maybe it was because he had been born and raised in Virginia and not a year went by that snow did not fall in the winter months. He had seen enough to last him several lifetimes and had certainly shoveled his fair share.

Suddenly he was jerked back in his seat as the old relic of a taxi came to a stop. He glanced back out the window and then back at the driver who stared at him with a look of impatience on his face. Lucas pulled out two twenty dollar American notes and handed them to the driver before grabbing his bag and exiting the cab. He had barely closed the door before the taxi went rocketing into the stream of traffic, leaving Lucas choking on the exhaust fumes.

Once inside the SVR building, his visitor's pass attached to his jacket, his pistol secured in a lockbox at reception, he was escorted down a long hallway, up two flights of stairs and through numerous passageways before they entered a small conference room. An older gentleman sat on one side of the table, appearing to be a seasoned vet, Lucas thought. He could always spot them right away—something about the way they held themselves, or perhaps it was the arrogance on their faces. He guessed this to be Director Vladimir Mishkin.

On the other side of the table sat a woman who he estimated was in her late twenties. Her hair was somewhere between a dark blond and a light brunette, and was held off her pale face with a tight chignon. They were both wearing suits, hers with a black skirt and plum blouse, sporting identification passes. They both stood as he entered.

"Special Agent Gates," the man stated as he held out his hand. "Director Vladimir Mishkin."

The Russian's hold was strong but not crushing. A man used to power, confident in his abilities. He squeezed the older man's hand before releasing it.

"I've been on the phone with your Agent in Charge Fitzgibbon. He advises me you are his best and that you understand the need to work quickly and quietly."

Lucas nodded. "I've been authorized to bring Ducane home. In any way possible."

Mishkin's eyes showed no surprise. "I suspected as such. The Russian Government has no issue with the extraction provided it is clean and there is no backlash on us."

"Thank you." He'd been expecting a little more resistance. Clearly the Russians wanted this dealt with just as much as the Americans did. He guessed Mishkin understood the tenuous ties that could unravel should Ducane succeed. Neither country wanted a war.

"We both want to avoid an international incident," Mishkin said, confirming what Lucas thought.

"Have you been able to pick up on any chatter?"

Mishkin's eyebrows pinched together in a frown. "Unfortunately, no. It's been unexpectedly quiet."

He rubbed his hand over the back of his neck. "Our analysts say the same."

"Which only serves to put me on edge. In my experience silence is often the most deadly."

"I agree." He glanced at the woman who'd yet to speak. She wasn't thin by Hollywood standards but had luscious curves a man could grab hold of. Her cheek bones were sharp and hinted at her heritage, giving her facial structure an unusual look, guaranteeing she got more than one passing glance by the male of the species.

Vladimir made a beckoning gesture with his hand and the woman stepped forward with a welcoming smile on her classically beautiful face. As she neared he saw her eyes were a cool grey framed with naturally dark lashes. He took a deep breath and his lungs filled with her flowery perfume, teasing him.

"Special Agent Gates I'd like you to meet Elena Ivanova," Mishkin introduced. "She'll be your agency liaison during your stay in Moscow. Any questions or complaints are to be directed through her."

He nodded at Elena. She was short compared to him, though most people were, standing several inches shorter than his six-foot. Her eye level matched Vladimir, who reminded him of a Hobbit—short and hairy.

Elena shook his hand. "How do you do?" she said in perfect English, with only a hint of an accent.

Lucas smiled back. "Well, thank you."

"Agent Ivanova will assist you in your endeavor. I hope to hear soon the situation has been neutralized," Mishkin said. "My agent will keep me informed of your progress."

Lucas shook the Director's hand again and waited until he'd left the conference room before turning towards the lovely Elena Ivanova.

"Shall we begin, Special Agent Gates?" she asked, her accent sending shivers down his spine.

"Please call me Lucas."

Elena nodded. "Very well, Lucas. You may address me as Elena."

"Elena," he said, letting her name roll off his tongue, tasting it.

He followed Elena down some more corridors, his full attention on the sway of her hips. It wasn't exaggerated as many women did when they knew a man was behind them but they still rocked side to side as they accommodated her long, fast stride. He yanked his gaze from her hips and ass, glancing inside some of the open office doors where agents were busy at work.

He could hear the drone of an overworked agent in the room up ahead. As they passed, he glanced into the room and saw the agent in charge giving instructions to a large group of men informing them about an approaching mission. Lucas knew the sight well, having been in the same position as the men many times before, so the language barrier was non-existent.

He leaned close to Elena and asked, "What mission are they about to impart on?"

He watched as her eyes widened and saw the question forming on her lips. He shook his head.

"No, the only other language I speak is body language."

"Oh," she nodded. "Well, you're correct. The agent is telling his men that his informant advised him the Mafiya has a shipment coming in on Tuesday. He wants to set up a perimeter around the dock with," she paused, listening intently to the man for a second before they were out of earshot. "Roughly fifty agents," she continued as they turned a corner.

Lucas gave off a quiet whistle. "Must be some shipment."

"It always is with the brotherhood."

She opened an office door and waited until he entered before closing it behind him. She walked around the side of her desk and sat down in her chair. He took the one reserved for visitors.

"Director Mishkin didn't give me many details as to why you're here, Special Agent Gates, only that I was to accommodate you in any way possible and should give you access to anything you want."

A non-work related thought popped into his head before he could stop it. He wasn't usually one to think of sex during an investigation, especially with a fellow agent. He was very goal orientated and believed an agent was an agent no matter their sex.

They were all trained for the same thing and knew their jobs. Each had their own specialty, their own worth. He wasn't a man with a big ego that needed to be stroked. He wasn't one to cause problems because his boss was a woman. He actually had a high esteem of women in elevated positions, admiring them greatly. He knew they had to bust their balls and be better than everybody else to get where they were and that kind of agent had his support one hundred percent. Which was why he didn't understand this reaction he had to Elena Ivanova.

Sure, she was beautiful but she wasn't the only attractive woman in the world. He liked to keep things on a professional level always. His break-up must have been affecting him more than he'd like to admit. Maybe it was his body or mind's way of telling him he was ready to settle down. God, he hoped not. He loved his life just as it was and he doubted there would be a woman alive who could understand and accept his career.

He nodded. "Good to hear." He settled himself more comfortably in his chair. "Two days ago there was a murder in the States, a professional hit. The man's name was Igor Zimtovich."

Elena frowned. "A Russian citizen?"

Again, he nodded. "That's not all. This was found on his remains."

He pulled out Igor's credentials and passed them to her. Her eyes widened when she opened it and caught sight of the SVR ID and badge. Her grey gaze met his, lips parted in surprise or shock.

"An SVR agent?"

"It gets worse. We uncovered some partial fingerprints which we were able to match to a Michael Ducane. An American terrorist. His specialty is bomb making."

Elena frowned. "Michael Ducane?"

"A seasoned terrorist and not to be taken lightly," he warned. "We believe he's currently in Russia. The target is unknown. Ducane goes where the money is. He's only part of the problem. I'm here to bring him in before he can do any damage and while I'm at it, find out who hired him and for what purpose."

"That's an awful lot to ask of one agent," she commented.

He grinned. "I enjoy a challenge."

"Most men do," she replied, her mouth curved on one side in what he hoped was amusement. "I'll see what I can do to help."

She jerked the mouse of her computer until the SVR seal and log-in boxes appeared on screen. He shifted in his seat to get a better view of the screen as she deftly she entered her username and password into fields and pressed enter. SVR's computer database came up, and she clicked on an icon and flicked through multiple screens before she had the one she wanted.

Lucas stared at the screen with the Russian characters and sank back in his chair waiting for her to tell him what her agency had on Ducane. Elena typed in a set of commands and Ducane's passport photo appeared on the screen. She twisted the monitor stand so he could more easily see her computer screen and read the information displayed.

"Ducane used an alias to enter the country which has since been flagged. He passed through our security twenty minutes before the alert to be on the lookout came through. He was, however, identified leaving a Moscow hotel at ten-fifty last night. The Marriot Hotel security camera caught him on tape meeting with Alvin Pochenchov." He sent her a questioning look. "He's one of our most elusive weapons dealers. He works freelance and plays at being an entrepreneur at his many nightclubs. SVR arrived a few minutes later but neither Ducane nor Pochenchov were found."

Damn it. The slimy bastard slipped through the cracks. They might as well give him a police escort to wherever he wanted to go. How could one man keep evading them? He wanted to hit something.

"No offense. But you have a known terrorist enter your country and no red flags go up?"

Elena frowned. "Are you joking? There's a summit this month in St. Petersburg. It may as well be Grand Central Station. So many internationals coming and going, we don't have the resources to do in-depth background checks on all of them."

Lucas nodded, understanding. They were fighting an uphill battle and the bad guys outnumbered them ten to one. The moment they took one out, another rose to take his place.

"Forgive me, I'm just frustrated and—"

"I'm the nearest person," she said, finishing his sentence. "It's all right. I understand the pressure you're under. It can't be easy being in your shoes."

"Thank you. I appreciate all your help."

She smiled and stood. "I haven't helped you yet. Coffee?"

Chapter 8

There was something about Lucas Gates that caught Elena's eye and had her thinking of candles and satin sheets. She had caught herself staring at his large hands more than once, at his long fingers with clean short nails. Embarrassed, she blushed, blood heating her cheeks until she was sure they were a rosy red.

She had only just met the man, which to her, made everything she was feeling so much worse. It had been a long time since any man had brought this particular response to her body, which was what had surprised her the most and made her pay attention. She had noticed men in the past, even after Nikolai's death. After all, her pulse still throbbed and her blood still ran hot, but not one pair of startling beautiful blue eyes, strong broad shoulders, or even one extremely tight bottom had caused every nerve ending in her body to sit up and take notice.

Over the past few months her friends had tried to get her to start dating again, but she wasn't ready.

She didn't think she would ever be. She had loved with all her heart, and now Nikolai was dead. She was sure her heart had followed him. Had she had her one chance at love, and now that it was gone would she be lonely for the rest of her life?

Her gaze flicked over the form of Lucas Gates once again, at his ruffled hair and creased clothes. What was it with the man that had her so out of sorts? What was he doing to her that made her so crazy and warm?

He caught her assessing gaze and her stomach did a somersault. She quickly redirected her interest elsewhere. He didn't appear to notice the electric charge that arced between them and she worried about what was happening to her. She swallowed, her mouth dry, and prayed her hormone surge would soon pass.

As much as she would like to get to know Lucas more, she couldn't. She was in a bad place with her emotions as it was. Adding a relationship—any type of relationship—into the mix would prove volatile. Besides, he had a job to do and soon he would return to the United States and she would never see him again. It would be best if she stopped thinking about him altogether. Now all she had to do was get her brain and libido to cooperate.

"What do you have on this Pochenchov?" Lucas asked, and she was glad for the interruption in her thoughts.

She took the last sip of coffee from her mug.

"Alvin Pochenchov was born here in Moscow in the early sixties and has sold over a million dollars' worth of weapons to a variety of terrorist groups and criminal organizations as well as mercenaries and small militia. So far, he has eluded arrest. He is well-known for his ability to obtain high end military grade weapons."

"That's quite a bio. Why is he still a free man?"

Elena sent him a dark look. "He's good at not being seen. Much like your Ducane, I'd say," she replied, her voice one octave above a snarl.

She didn't like his insinuation that the law enforcement in her country was too inept or corrupt not to be able to bring down one man.

"Ouch," he said, with a grin. "Touché."

"I'm sure even in your country there are men who pay their way out of trouble, that or threaten and kill to stay out of prison. He has no qualms about doing whatever he has to, to remain a free man. It's always about what we can prove and not what we think or know."

"Same shit, different country. I know all too well," he admitted. "Where does he get his weapons from?"

"He pays to have them smuggled off army bases here in Russia, Georgia, and the Ukraine. You name it, he gets it and sells it to you at double the price he paid."

"Talk about inflation," Lucas commented.

Elena nodded. "What kind of supplies will Ducane be requiring? It may give us an estimate of time. The harder to acquire, the more time we might have."

He gave her a look that seemed to say he liked the way she thought.

"Unfortunately, his shopping list is pretty easy to

come by, if you have the contacts—which he clearly has," Lucas stated. "Do you have a list of Pochenchov's clients? Maybe we can cross reference the names to those previously connected with Ducane."

"How would that help?"

"I don't know. I'm grasping at straws. Ducane has never worked in Russia before and I want to know who put him in contact with Pochenchov. Maybe we can squeeze him for information. Or it might lead us to whoever hired Ducane."

Elena nodded, following his line of reasoning. "I wish I could help you, but all of Pochenchov's known contacts and clients are currently serving multiple life sentences in maximum security prisons. Prisons here in Russia have very little perks which don't include phone calls or internet. They have no contact with the outside world. Setting up a meeting between a supplier and a buyer would be out of the question."

Lucas huffed out a deep breath.

"So we have an arms dealer in Russia, a dead SVR agent and a known terrorist. I don't think it could get any worse than that. I guess Zimtovich could've been the connection between Ducane and Pochenchov," he wondered aloud.

Elena typed Igor Zimtovich into her search engine. "You're assuming that Agent Zimtovich wasn't there on a sanctioned mission. Perhaps he was merely following Ducane and was caught."

Lucas raised an eyebrow. "Is that what your computer is telling you?"

Elena read the file on her computer screen. She

frowned as confusion set in.

"What?" Lucas asked.

"I don't understand. Agent Zimtovich was working as a liaison between the SVR and the FSB, another one of our agencies," she elaborated. "There is no reason at all he should have left Russia and it isn't the place of a liaison officer to go flitting about the world. We are always to remain in-house, so to speak."

"Tell me, who was the agent assigned to the Pochenchov case? Assuming you have agents monitoring him and building cases against him," he added.

"This may be Russia, Special Agent Gates, but we do try to put away the bad guy. Of course our resources are very limited and have a budget nowhere in the range of the CIA, but we do our best."

He grimaced. "I've offended you again. I apologize. And it's Lucas, remember?"

She gave a sharp nod. "We don't have twenty-four hour surveillance, but an Agent would have been assigned. It's his or her job to gather intel and bring him down."

"Would I be able to talk to him? See if he had noticed anything in the past, give me a few leads. It couldn't hurt."

"No, it couldn't," she agreed. "I'll get that name for you." She turned back to her computer and again her fingers flew across the keyboard. A moment later, a file appeared on her screen and she scrolled down and stiffened.

"Nikolai Nagregor," she said, her voice barely

above a whisper.

She couldn't go a day without thinking of Nikolai, to remember the life they had and how that life had ended so abruptly. He had been the love of her life. That love was gone, and only memories were left. Good memories, but memories didn't keep a woman warm at night.

She thought back to just a little while ago, the fantasies she'd had of Lucas and her lying naked between heated sheets and suddenly she felt guilty. It was like cold water had just been poured over her head and she felt the urge to roll up into a ball and cry. It was an unreasonable emotion and that Nikolai himself wouldn't blame her. He would encourage her to move on with her life, to find someone she could love with all her heart. But she couldn't. Not this soon. She could still remember the feel of Nikolai beside her, kissing her, touching her. The smell of his skin and the sound of his voice.

"You know him?"

Yes, she knew him. Nikolai. Her Nikolai. She remembered the first day she had met him. He had been assigned as her supervisor when she had begun working for SVR. His dark hair had streaks of grey even at thirty. She had fallen for him, hard and fast and completely. No other man had compared to him. And he had loved her. God, he had loved her and she him. She had never felt more loved by anyone than she had by Nikolai. He had broken the rules for her, asking her out on a date. Agents were discouraged from becoming familiar with one another. But Nikolai hadn't cared. Never would she forget the way he had devoured her with his eyes, the molten heat in his dark gaze that had liquefied her insides as he had asked her out to dinner.

"That wouldn't be such a good idea," she had replied. "Isn't dating within the agency frowned upon?"

Nikolai had shrugged. "I make my own rules and sooner or later, Elena Ivanova, I always get what I want. Something you should know, since I want you."

It hadn't been a threat but a promise. Her whole body had shook with desire. He had hounded her into complying every time he saw her, until one day she had said yes. He had taken her to a nice romantic restaurant before walking her home and kissing her goodnight, the perfect gentleman. Within two years, they had married.

Now, she nodded. "He was my husband," she said simply.

She saw shock on his face before it was replaced with something she couldn't identify. Disappointment? His gaze dropped to her left hand, at the ring adorned with a diamond on her finger, and she self-consciously twisted the gold band around and around as she always did in highly stressful situations. The action typically soothed her, a tenuous link to her husband, but today all it seemed to do was add to her apprehension.

"Was?" he asked, studying her face closely.

Elena nodded stiffly. "He's dead."

Shot. Murdered. Gone.

She turned away from Lucas, out her office window. Small snowflakes continued to fall. They were in for a cold front settling over the city. A sharp pain stabbed at her in the vicinity of her heart, a pain that never really went away but was merely hidden, buried deep beneath her grief, her guilt at arriving too late, at not being able to avenge him and find his killer.

"I'm sorry." His tone was genuine and she saw sympathy in his eyes.

"As am I, but I thank you for your kind words."

She smiled and once again thought what a kind and sincere man he was, and chided herself for wandering into forbidden territory again. Guilt once more flooded her body and she was ashamed at her wayward thoughts. In her heart she was still married and loathed her attraction to Lucas. It had only taken the mention of her husband for her to feel disloyal and she wished with all her heart she didn't find Lucas appealing. Nikolai had only been gone six months, but to Elena it felt like a lifetime. The pain of loss tugged more deeply now than when she had discovered his body.

Torn, she brought her mind back to the matter at hand.

"Nikolai was a good agent. Hardworking. Dedicated. He took on the worst of the worst. He wanted to leave the world a little better than when he came into it."

"Sounds like a good man," he commented.

"He was."

"When did he die?" he asked softly, his gaze drifting once more to her anxious fingers that unconsciously twisted her wedding ring. She caught herself and clasped her hands tightly together in an effort to stop.

"Six months ago."

"How?"

She frowned at the question. "He was killed," she replied, finding it difficult to force the word out of her mouth.

Lucas leaned back in his chair and contemplated. "Your husband's death seems awfully convenient for Pochenchov," he noted.

Don't get me started, she thought. She had been down that road before. Pochenchov was one of her top suspects in Nikolai's murder.

"A lot of people benefited from Nikolai's death—a lot of bad people," she said. Tears threatening to spill as they always did when she thought of Nikolai's short life. "Nikolai kept scrupulous records. I doubt he could've told you more than what is in this file. I'll be happy to translate it for you."

"I appreciate that. I think in the meantime, I might do some recon. See if I can't track this Pochenchov down."

"And what do you plan on doing if you happen to stumble across him?" Elena asked, concerned. Pochenchov is one mean S-O-B from what she'd heard and the idea of Lucas facing off against him didn't sit well.

"I think I'll ask him where Ducane is," Lucas replied simply and much too casually. His eyes held a gleam that told her he was looking forward to it.

"And what makes you think he'd tell you?"

"I'm a very persuasive man, Elena."

She smiled. "Of that I have no doubt. Be careful,

Special Agent Gates. I hear Pochenchov isn't a very nice man," she warned.

"That's okay," he told her. "The same has been said about me from time to time."

"This isn't the United States, Lucas. Good agents don't seem to live long here. If you need anything, here is my card."

She produced a card from the pocket of her suit jacket and handed it to him.

"Thank you, and I promise you I will be careful."

He collected his coat from the back of the visitor's chair and walked out the door, leaving Elena to clean up the files. She couldn't believe her luck. Of the thousands of agents in the building, her case had to involve Nikolai.

***

Half an hour later, Elena was filing away a folder into her file cabinet when there was a knock on her door which was immediately opened by Agent Alexei Dimitrovich. He wore a black suit and a white dress shirt. Of all the years she had known him, she had never seen him in anything but. No jeans, no polos, just suit pants and dress shirts. His dark hair had been combed and parted to one side. He was a handsome man, but she had never looked at him that way. He had always been overshadowed by Nikolai in her eyes, and after Nikolai's death he had been too close a friend to consider him romantically. Not that she had ever thought of pursuing him, but she could see his allure to other women.

Alexei had been Nikolai's best friend. They had met at the Academy and bonded instantly. He had also been the best man at her and Nikolai's wedding and after Nikolai had been murdered, he had taken it upon himself to make sure she kept her sanity. A tough job considering what a basket case she had been. She was grateful to him for that. After all, she wasn't the only one who had lost Nikolai.

"Elena," he greeted, his calculating gaze sweeping her office as if expecting the entire Red Army to be camped behind her desk. "Am I interrupting anything?"

Elena shook her head as she made her way to greet him. "No, I'm just cleaning up."

Alexei smiled and gave her a quick hug. She was always his friend first and a fellow agent second. "How are you?"

His dark eyes bored into hers, daring her to lie to him. She had tried it once and had suffered the consequences. Since then she always told him the truth. She liked the fact he cared enough to call her out on her lies when all she had wanted was to be left alone with her pain.

"I'm fine, Alexei, really. Thank you."

And she was. She would never get over losing her husband. She would never stop loving him and still felt angry at the thought he'd been taken from her far too early. They'd had so little time together.

Life sucks and then you die.

Nikolai's favorite saying passed through her head. He had often said those six words to her when life didn't go their way. A hint of a smile moved her lips a fraction at the memory.

"In fact, I'm doing better," she continued, telling Alexei her good news. "Director Mishkin put me on a case this morning."

"Yes, I heard you drew the short straw with the American."

Her eyebrow rose. "You are well informed. Especially for someone who doesn't work for this agency."

Alexei shrugged. "It's my job, Elena."

"Since when have I been your job, Alexei?"

He watched her closely to the point where she was starting to feel uncomfortable under his scrutiny. "Since the day Nikolai died. I know he would've wanted me to look after you," he said earnestly.

She exhaled deeply. "And I appreciate that, but I don't need someone looking out for me. I really am doing better and I doubt he would want you to look after me for the rest of your life, Alexei. You need to move on as well, and get your own life away from me."

Alexei was one of the few people who had seen her at her worst. After Nikolai had been murdered, she had been a mess, determined to prove his death was no coincidence. She and Alexei had never been true friends. They had just put up with one another because they both cared about Nikolai. After his death, they had mourned him together.

"Yes, well, let's not get into that now. It's certainly good to see you back working again. You were born for this job. Nikolai always said that and he was right. You look happy."

Elena smiled. Alexei never said anything he

didn't mean, so his observation was of the highest praise. "I've never stopped working."

She had been relegated to desk work, though. Her denial about Nikolai's death had caused some ripples.

"Paperwork doesn't count, Elena. My offer still stands. Anytime you want, you can come work for FSB. We could use a good liaison like you."

It was an offer he'd made countless times before, one she appreciated but would never accept. Despite the recent past, SVR was her home and yet another reminder of her life with Nikolai—one she wasn't in any hurry to leave.

"So tell me about this American," he suggested.

He sat down in the chair Lucas had vacated. She noticed Alexei sneered the word *American*. Elena sat down in her chair and regarded him from across her desk.

"Well, for starters, his name is Special Agent Lucas Gates not *American*, Alexei," she stated.

"Why is he here?"

"So you don't know everything?" She smiled at him. "He's just here to catch a wanted man who has slipped into the country."

She kept her information sparse. It was not that she didn't trust Alexei, but rather it was none of his business. If there was anything Nikolai had taught her it was to keep things close to the chest and everything was need to know. Alexei didn't need to know. She had always listened to Nikolai's advice, which he'd learned from previous mistakes, and she had no desire to experience them firsthand herself. If you expected to live, you paid attention to what those more knowledgeable had to say. You didn't become a seasoned agent by walking around with blinders on.

Alexei nodded. "Well, you be careful. Those Americans are loose cannons, so used to making up their own laws. I'd hate for his actions to come back at you." He prepared to leave. "My advice to you is to keep him on a short leash, Elena."

She contained her urge to roll her eyes. Alexei had always been anti-American, often spouting off insults at the country. Russia had a love-hate relationship with the United States, often in competition. She escorted him to the door. "Thank you for your concern, Alexei, but I can handle it."

"Just looking out for you," he told her.

"And I appreciate it. I always do."

He pressed a chaste goodbye kiss to her cheek. Then she closed the door firmly behind him.

Chapter 9

Lucas was well in his element as he entered the seedy nightclub. He may not speak the language but he had other equally important gifts, ones that could not be ignored, even by the most heinous of creatures. And Lucas had met many of them since he'd left Elena's office.

It hadn't taken him long to find out where Alvin Pochenchov spent his time. All he had to do was ask the right person the right question and here he was standing before one of the many nightclubs on Tverskaya Street, the trendiest area for tourists and Russians alike. It was also the most expensive street to shop on throughout Russia, but he didn't plan on paying for the information he was shopping for. He didn't buy coincidence, and Agent Nagregor's death seemed much too tidy for him.

As he entered Pochenchov's club, he glanced about, noting the position and threat level of each patron, scanning their clothes for bulges that concealed hidden weapons. His eyes barely skimmed over the many female dancers dressed scantily in little pink panties and nothing else, their breasts on display for all to admire and ogle.

The dancers on stage were moving provocatively, some making love to the poles before them, sliding up and down while maintaining eye contact with their marks. Lucas could never understand what men saw in coming to places like these. To look upon women jaded in their lives, showing their well-used bodies for a buck. Lucas liked mystery and romance. He liked to use his imagination when it came to women. To imagine what she was wearing under her clothes, to wonder whether she wearing red panties or blue, cotton or silk, or if she'd been naughty today and wore none at all. A man could spend hours contemplating such things, like he had earlier today in Elena's office. He couldn't help himself.

Between her grey eyes and tempting supple body, he'd had a hard enough time not giving into his Neanderthal urges by throwing her to the floor and having his way with her. There was something about Elena that hit him hard in the stomach and had all other thoughts rushing out of his well-trained mind. She was unlike any woman he had ever met. Intriguing, beautiful, smart and sassy—a complete package. His heart had damn near stopped at the thought she was married. It had taken a few seconds for her words to fully penetrate his mind before he realized she'd said *was*.

He'd almost rejoiced at the possibility that once the case was closed they'd acknowledge their mutual attraction, the air between them charged and crackling with energy, but despite her widow status it was clear to him Elena Ivanova was still very much married to her husband. Nagregor must've been one hell of a man for Elena to continue to hold a candle for him long after his death. An unexpected twinge of jealously shot through him. He envied the dead man.

Lucas's gaze swept the bar. A man in a tight black shirt showed off his impeccable six pack and pectorals while drying sturdy glasses, his attention on the wrestling match playing on the widescreen TV above the bar. Lucas moved over to the bar and sat down, allowing his gaze to settle on the wrestlers. He wasn't one for watching sport games—preferring to be part of the action rather than the spectator—but he wanted more time to check out the establishment before making his move.

Lucas indicated to the bartender with a jerk of his head and the man poured two fingers of vodka into a glass he'd just finished cleaning and placed it on the scarred wood of the bar. It was the type of business that served only two types of drink and what you were given you drank without comment. Lucas put the glass to his lips and swallowed the liquid fire as he surveyed the darkened room, lit only by neon lights.

To an observer he looked like an ordinary American tourist, out for a good night—a few drinks and a lap dance to warm his chilled body. One of many they would see come and go through the months. None saw just how sharp his eyes were, how intelligent and shrewd he was, and how he built a map of the nightclub in his head, marking the exits and obstacles, making sure he had a plan B in case the first went askew.

How gaudy, Lucas thought with disgust as he lay down money on the bar, placing his empty glass on top. The quintessential strip joint. Without giving away his avid interest, his gaze skimmed over the man in the corner booth. Two large bosomed women hung onto his every word, giggling every so often while stroking the man high on his thighs.

Two large, thick armed, broad-chested men stood to the side. They wore the same black shirt as the man behind the bar, matched with black trousers and shoes. They wore identical expressions that would strike fear in any man's heart and if any fool failed to be fearful, the large caliber weapons clipped to their belts would surely do the trick. Lucas was unimpressed. He had seen scarier men.

He stood and stared directly at the man who was gleefully lapping up his female companions' attentions. His hairy hand—gleaming as the light hit the gems in his oversized rings—slid up from one woman's waist to her large double D breast and squeezed possessively. Lucas's mouth curled at the disgusting display as he strode across the floor purposefully. The two goons went on instant alert, their bodies stiffening in preparation for action.

Lucas kept his eyes on Alvin Pochenchov, dismissing each guard as nothing but a small barrier he had yet to get through, but didn't anticipate an issue. With one swift motion, he grabbed one by the wrist, applying pressure to certain crucial points and dropped him to the floor without exerting any effort whatsoever. The second man pulled a knife from the small of his back and swished the blade back and forth through the air. Lucas moved deftly and side-stepped each strike, one barely missing his abdomen. His hands were fists, raised high on his chest, protecting his heart as he waited patiently for the moment to strike.

Pochenchov's man was cocky, believing himself to have the upper hand. Lucas could tell the man had no formal training, his movements too slow, too unrefined. He may be a large man, but he knew nothing of wielding a knife properly. Lucas was soon to teach him that having a sharp blade meant nothing; one first needed to know how to use it before trying to end a life with it.

Lucas pivoted about on his foot, and had in short order broken the gorilla of a man's wrist, the knife he had favored falling to the ground, useless and out of reach. Within seconds, Lucas finished him off with a headlock, cutting the air supply off and rendering him unconscious. He fell to the floor with a loud thud.

Alvin Pochenchov had obviously, after tearing himself away from more pleasurable pursuits, seen how ineffective his men were and was in the process of reaching for his gun when Lucas produced his Glock and aimed it right at Pochenchov's heavily beating heart.

"Drop it," he ordered in a voice no one would dare to disobey.

Gingerly, Alvin tossed his weapon to the floor. It slid along the smooth surface and came to a stop beside the unconscious bodyguard.

Alvin swore with gusto, no doubt calling Lucas

everything from a bastard of a whore to the son of Satan. Of course, he couldn't be sure. But if the rapid fire Russian was anything to go by, it certainly wasn't a lullaby. Lucas admired the lengthy tirade. It meant he had inconvenienced Pochenchov, and the man would be more than happy to part with information for the simple delight of being rid of him.

"Are you done?" he asked idly as he retrieved his badge from his pocket and flashed it to Alvin. "Special Agent Gates," he identified himself.

As he glared up at Lucas, Pochenchov's rounded stomach protruded heavily over the waistband of his pants, placing great pressure on his belt and zipper. He was a man of leisure who thought of nothing but his own pleasure.

Alvin sneered. "What do you want, American?" He practically spat the words, his lip curling in distaste as if he had just swallowed something foul. His eyes were narrowed and he was looking like he would enjoy killing Lucas. That was fine, he would enjoy killing Pochenchov, but first he wanted information and wanted it now.

Lucas's gaze didn't leave his, showing him no fear. He was there for a reason and he wasn't leaving until he had all his questions answered. "Information on Michael Ducane."

Pochenchov feigned ignorance. "I know no Ducane."

Lucas shook his head. "See, that's not what I've heard. Now listen up, scumbag. We know Ducane met with you yesterday. I want to know where I can find him and whether you've already delivered his supplies."

Two dark eyes pinned him. Lucas could see the ruthless man beneath the greasy exterior. Lucas had dealt many times with men like Pochenchov over the years and knew they were ruled by money and greed and nothing else. There was no such thing as loyalty and friendship in their world.

"You better be careful, American. Going around asking questions that are none of your business, you'll end up in landfill."

He shrugged. He wasn't overly concerned with the Russian's threats. "I'm not too worried."

"You should be. You see, I have insurance which is why I am not in prison like some of my other associates. So beware, American. I have friends in high places. Higher in the government than even you. I could make you disappear."

"And I bet all I have to do is tell some of your 'colleagues' that you're sitting here enjoying yourself with Federal insurance while they're rotting in a maximum security prison and we'll see how long you survive."

Pochenchov's dark eyes darkened even more until they were almost black in his head. His face turned red with rage and Lucas could see the vein in his temple pulsating with an effort to control his temper. To a layman, he would seem quite calm. Lucas was no layman. He knew letting his guard down now was tantamount to suicide.

"You certainly have a way with bargaining, American. What is it you want to know?"

What didn't he want to know?

He wanted to know where Ducane had gone,

what the target was, and how long he had. He wanted to know where Zimtovich fit in and what he could've told Ducane that was worth his life. He wanted to know what happened to Elena's husband. Why did he feel as if Nikolai Nagregor had been involved directly and indirectly with everything up to this point? He opened his mouth, ready to ask the first question but instead another one came out.

"Do you know a man named Nagregor, an agent for SVR?"

Pochenchov nodded. "Of course. He was the SVR agent who was murdered six months back. He stuck his nose where it didn't belong also. Perhaps you should take his death as a lesson, American, and do what he should have done."

"And what was that?" Lucas asked mildly, as if he cared what Pochenchov thought he should do.

The man lit a thick cigar and took a deep puff, filling the already smoky club with the potent stench. "Back off."

"Did you have him killed?" Lucas demanded, ignoring Pochenchov's advice.

He chuckled. "Do you really expect me to answer that, American? Even we here in Russia have a court system. But I admit I respected the man. He could not be bought or threatened. I don't come across integrity very often. No." He shook his head. "I did not have him killed. I didn't have to. Nagregor was a dead man from the moment he discovered something he shouldn't have."

Now we were getting somewhere. Everyone wanted to talk. Even the most hardened criminals find it hard not to boast. "And what might that be?"

"That there is a mole inside Russian Intelligence. You think the Russians cannot find me?" he laughed. "They do not look for me."

Lucas dived out the way as the bullet from a gun whizzed past his head, barely missing him. He hit the floor hard, jarring his bones, even as he aimed his weapon. He didn't watch where the bullet landed. It wasn't his main concern at the moment. As long as he wasn't hit, he didn't care. Screams surrounded him, blocking out any other sound he might hear. The dancers had dropped to the floor of the stage, too frightened to move any farther, waiting until the last bullet was fired. The nightclub's patrons, unsure of what to do or what was happening and why, moved in every direction, creating confusion while rushing for the exit.

Two more gunshots sounded. Lucas watched as one bullet hit Pochenchov in the head. His body slumped back in his chair, his eyes open and sightless. Lucas moved slowly and silently amidst the flurry of activity, keeping low to the ground, out of sight. He stopped behind an empty chair, using it as cover. He leveled his gun in the direction of the shooter, his analytical brain having already determined where the shots had originated even while he had been under fire. From his position behind the chair, he applied pressure to the trigger of his gun. He heard the loud *boom*, smelled the burned gunpowder and felt the gun recoil. Years of training had him keeping his weapon pointed towards the danger instead of at the ceiling. The man in his sight jerked and dropped to the floor.

Lucas got to his feet, assessing the danger as he

crossed the floor and bent down beside Pochenchov. He didn't need to feel for a pulse. A neat round nine millimeter hole marred his forehead, blood and brain matter splattered against the wall behind him. Pochenchov hadn't had time to react.

Good riddance, he thought. One less asshole in the world. He stepped over towards the shooter, keeping his weapon trained on the man, waiting for signs of movement. He kicked away the shooter's Russian made semi-automatic MP-443 Grach pistol, a heavy feeling settling inside his stomach. Something was not right here. He knelt beside the body of the shooter and rummaged through his pockets. He pulled out a leather case and opened it to find an SVR badge.

Lucas heard the telltale cock behind him of a gun's safety being released. He let his pistol slide from his hand, holding onto it by just his index finger caught on the trigger guard. He raised his hands to his head and turned around slowly to face the MDV police officer standing there, his service pistol pointed at Lucas's chest.

The man dressed in a blue and red uniform spouted off Russian in rapid bursts, the words coming at him full force. Lucas held the man's gaze, wondering at the wisdom of his plan. Wasn't it written somewhere that when confronted with an angry dog, never look them in the eye, something about looking down at the ground in a subservient manner?

Too late to change my mind now. Might as well power on.

The folks around here all seemed to think that

every American was arrogant so he might as well live up to the stereotype. Not that he wasn't arrogant but he had earned it by working hard and knowing with confidence that he could back it up with his abilities. He spoke very calmly, never breaking eye contact with the MVD officer.

"I don't speak Russian. I'm CIA working with the SVR. Call them and check."

The officer glared, his mouth curling much like the dead Alvin Pochenchov's had. This was obviously not his day. Did anyone in this country not despise an American? The officer responded in a harsh voice, his English fragmented. "Put your weapon down!"

Bits of spittle flew at Lucas's face as the man spoke. He was tempted to step back out of range but had no idea how itchy the police officer's trigger finger was. He didn't want to take any unnecessary chances. He didn't want any bullet holes in his body. Lucas knew he was up shit creek if he didn't find a way out of this mess.

"I'm CIA. Check my coat pocket."

The officer made a threatening move forward. He spoke rapidly into his radio, most likely calling for back-up. He would probably only have another five minutes tops before he was arrested. He doubted the Russian court would rule in his favor— killing one of their agents and all. A bad agent, but he could hardly prove that now could he? He would be lucky to make it to prison before being beaten to death.

"You have no jurisdiction here. You are under arrest and your status will be decided after your case is reviewed," the police officer told him.

Things were going from bad to worse. He had to get the fuck out of there. His mind rapidly ran through various scenarios. The officer came toward him, handcuffs at the ready. This would not do. Lucas sprang to life as the officer moved even closer. He knocked the pistol from the officer's hand before raising his elbow into the man's face, breaking his nose. The officer grabbed hold of his nose, the blood gushing out. In a last ditch effort to retain his suspect, he pulled a knife from his uniform and came at Lucas with the sharp dagger.

Lucas tried to move away as he was attacked with the knife, the blade slicing the palm of his hand when he moved too slowly. He used his foot to trip the officer, knocking him on his ass before escaping to the street and losing himself in the crowd of late evening partiers and shoppers.

He didn't like to think it, but he was currently up shit creek. He wasn't stupid. The Russian Government would convict him before they would even look at their own. Everything was slowly falling together and he knew he'd been set up. But he wasn't about to take that sitting down. Someone from within the government was calling the shots and he wasn't playing nice.

He needed help, needed to contact Jim and explain what happened and get Jim to run interference with Director Mishkin while they organized his extraction. There was nothing worse than being stuck in a foreign country with no bag and no passport to get out. Both were in Elena's office at SVR Headquarters in Yasenevo. There was no way of getting to them without being caught and possibly killed. He doubted he'd get a fair trial, let alone be given time to explain his actions.

Worse, he was without his gun, having left it in Pochenchov's nightclub as he made his escape. He was a dead man walking and he knew it—a marked man. His ego wasn't big enough to be bruised by admitting he needed help. The life of a CIA Special Agent couldn't afford such stupid frivolities. He would take anything he could get. Only problem was, where could he go for help without fear of being shot?

He crossed the street, moving at a brisk pace. He could hear the emergency vehicles stopping outside Pochenchov's nightclub. It would be all over the news soon. He needed to get someplace safe. Somewhere he could think and regroup.

An image of Elena popped into his head—lovely Elena, all creamy skin and silky hair, smelling of gardenias. He had never thought much about a woman's perfume, but hers along with the rest of her had been a constant thought in the back of his head. Even with the last couple of hours he had just endured, the thought of her brought a smile to his face.

Elena.

Lucas didn't want to involve her. He would do anything not to have to drag her into this mess he made. She didn't need that and she certainly didn't deserve it. She was the only one who had helped him since he'd arrived in Moscow. But she was his only chance. He only prayed she was who she seemed to be.

He pulled out the card she had given him from his coat pocket. Elena's name was typed proudly on the front in Russian Cyrillic characters along with her office numbers. He would only use them in case of emergency. He would like to avoid that option if he could. Now that he had a starting point, he was feeling slightly better, and the knot in his stomach stopped tightening inside of him. Next stop was a phone booth.

White Pages is worldwide, right?

Chapter 10

Michael Ducane smiled when he heard the news of Alvin Pochenchov's demise. He sat at an old oak desk in a small farmhouse west of St. Petersburg. He was glad the CIA Special Agent had finished him off. It saved him time killing the Russian bastard once his job was completed and it got the Special Agent off his back for a while.

It was clear he was the reason the agent was in Russia. Agent Zimtovich's body had obviously been discovered and now a full investigation was underway. He must be extra careful from now on, ensuring he didn't make any stupid mistakes. It would also be a good thing to keep his head down, at least for now. He had no plans of being captured anytime soon, if ever.

It was a good thing he had gotten the shipment from Pochenchov when he had. He didn't have time to find another weapons dealer. Especially one that was so well connected. Despite Pochenchov's slimy demeanor, he had certainly come through with the goods.

He cut the malleable plasticized adhesive of C4 into a large block and added it to the small pile he'd already prepared. The top quality C4 was one of the many items requested that had come from Alvin's black market dealers, most likely courtesy of the Russian Army.

The C4 was made up of RDX explosive and plasticizer. The small compound was often used in professional fields and is more powerful than TNT, gunpowder, or dynamite. In the past he had worked with all types of explosives, using whatever he could get his hands on. Now he had the luxury of choosing even the most expensive or elusive chemicals to create the type of devastation he wanted.

He would've preferred to have used the RDX to make his own cocktail, one he could perfect and put his name to, but his time was limited and he had to make do with the already prepared C4. Now all he had to do was tweak the quantity until he had the right size blast that would penetrate the thick barrier between him and his targets.

He liked the fact he held lives in his hands. It was a thrill to decide who lived and who died and he'd never once missed watching his bombs detonate. He'd never felt so alive as he watched the panic break out after his explosion. There was no feeling like it.

He wiped his hands on his clothes, unconcerned about leaving explosive residue on his clothes or person. His benefactor had ensured he had an escort past the guards and the dogs that were trained to smell explosive chemicals, not that it was supposed to be an issue. The scent dogs, he'd been informed, would be useless on that day as a precaution. *They'd better be*, he thought. Otherwise, his plans would crumble.

He added the negative and positive wires needed into the block and tested the signal from his remote to the metal panel attached to the C4. The light flicked green, stating it was ready for a trial run before he switched the receiver off. He had done this many times before.

He picked up the white rectangular slabs of C4 he'd prepared and took them outside. He stomped through the thick snow covering the ground and placed the charge inside the nearby barn and set the timer for three minutes. He turned away and casually made his way back the porch of the farmhouse and turned to watch the force of the bomb as it exploded. He needed to make sure the blast area was sufficient. If not, he would have to modify the quantity until it was. The force of the explosion shook the farmhouse, the glass of the windows rattling slightly before shattering. He nodded to himself as he took in the fire that engulfed what was left of the barn.

He shivered through his thick woolen coat and long johns.

Jesus, this is an unholy place.

He vowed this would be the first and only time he would take a job in Russia. He didn't like freezing his ass off in the middle of nowhere. He stepped inside the farmhouse and shook off the snow from his jacket, swearing as a snowflake fell down his shirt opening and slid down his back. He had a little more work to do here. Then, with any luck, forty-eight hours from now he would be on a flight to his next commission.

Chapter 11

Elena was exhausted. She'd spent the previous evening in Director Mishkin's office, being subjected to his tirade about 'that American' and how he had better be apprehended shortly. She'd never seen Vladimir so angry and here she thought she pushed his buttons. She had nothing on Agent Gates. Elena had been happy to see the back of his door. She had decided to work through the rest of the night and finish up her reports and take the day off. The sun was just beginning to rise above the tall buildings as she lifted her knees higher to accommodate for the night's snowfall.

What had Lucas gotten himself into? There was no way he would get out of this. If she was Lucas, she would be getting herself to the nearest airport and flying back home. Let the politicians and agency heads smooth over troubled waters; that was what they were there for.

She had walked to the Metro station in Yasenevo and boarded the train on the Kaluzhsko-Rizhskaya line and headed home. After changing trains farther on down the line and walking in the early morning's cold air, she was ready for a hot shower and climbing into bed to fall into a long, deep slumber.

Elena shivered as she made her way towards her apartment in Pushkinskaya. She could feel the cold temperature seeping through her winter clothes as the day promised to be a cold one. At seven-thirty it was only minus one point six degrees, set to continue dropping throughout the day. A good day to stay home snuggled in bed with a good book and a steaming cup of hot chocolate. She ambled up the stairs of the apartment building she had once shared with her husband and finally reached her floor. She walked over to her door and fiddled through her purse looking for her key.

"Don't you know you should already have your key ready before you get to your door?" a voice asked her from behind. Startled, she spun around and stared in shock at Lucas who was huddled in the dark crevice opposite her door.

"What the hell are you doing here?" she whispered. "Every SVR agent is out looking for you. Not to mention the MDV. You're an extremely popular man."

Lucas stepped forward into the light of the corridor. His hair was tousled, his scarf hanging down at an odd angle and the rumpled clothes he wore yesterday now sported dirt and blood. He looked like he'd had a rough night. The lines on his face had deepened and his eyes were bloodshot. She tried not to feel anything towards him but her heart softened and she knew she'd relent.

"You're my liaison," he said simply.

Elena shook her head. "I think it's a deal breaker when you shoot an SVR agent. They have witnesses, Special Agent Gates. The SVR are looking at this as a direct hit on Russia. Director Mishkin has been ranting all night about you. I'm afraid he has informed Special Agent in Charge Fitzgibbon about your circumstances."

Lucas rubbed the back of his neck with his hand. "The agent shot Alvin Pochenchov. I'm a witness. I only shot him to defend myself. He never identified himself as an SVR agent."

Elena sighed heavily, her voice weary. "Alvin Pochenchov is a known criminal. The agent could have a number of reasons for shooting him. If he indeed did."

"He did," Lucas interrupted firmly.

"Very well, he didn't identify himself," Elena agreed, reasonably. "Still you should have allowed yourself to be brought in, asked them to contact me instead of running. It looks like you're as guilty as sin."

"Shit, Elena, surely you don't believe that? I'm being set up."

"Of course I don't believe that. You're a very honest man, Lucas. If I know anything at all, it is that." She rubbed her brow in frustration and weariness. "What a mess. Didn't your mother ever tell you never to piss in someone else's pool?"

***

Lucas smiled, somehow not expecting such a phrase to come from Elena's mouth. To him, it sounded downright hilarious. It was the first time he'd smiled since leaving her office the day before.

"She did, but it never stuck. I'm sorry, Elena. I hate to involve you but I really need your help. Please," he added for good measure. He was desperate and if she didn't help him, he didn't have a clue what his next move would be.

Elena stared at him for a long while, just enough for his heart to sink before she let out a deep sigh and a whispered expletive. He didn't need to know the translation to understand it was directed at him, or his situation.

"Come on," she said as she unlocked her apartment door and led him inside.

The apartment was cozy. The heater had taken the chill out of the air. Her furniture was sparse, not over-crowding the small space, but completely feminine. The room was done in pinks and white lace and Lucas wondered if Nikolai had felt emasculated here or if it was just him. It took a very secure man to live here. There were a few paintings on the wall and several photographs over the old-fashioned fireplace, adding life to the room. He noticed Elena had no time for plants or flowers.

She hung her coat up in the closet and turned to face him. Her eyes softened. He knew he must look terrible. He'd had little sleep while waiting for her, constantly moving to keep his blood flowing as the temperature dropped significantly. He ran his hand through his hair in an effort to tidy himself up and winced as he jostled his wounded hand where the knife had sliced through skin and blood had dried.

"You're hurt. I'll get something to clean you up

with."

She walked down the hall to where he supposed her bathroom was. Once again, his gaze swept across the room. The apartment was everything his was not. It was the type of place you wanted to come home to after a long day's work. Warm and inviting, altogether homey. Of course, the fact Elena was there could also be attributed to that.

The photos on the fireplace mantle drew his attention. He could see a smiling Elena standing next to a handsome man. He assumed this was her husband Nikolai. He reached out and picked up the wedding photo, his curiosity piqued. In the photo, Elena was decked out in a fashionable white, simply designed but perfectly rendered wedding dress. The sunlight danced off her wedding ring, causing a multitude of colors to shine through the diamond.

Nikolai was as dashing as any man could in his black suit, his obsidian hair and eyes adding to the allure of the tall, dark and handsome stereotype. His arm was wrapped possessively around Elena's waist. Two men stood on either side of Elena and Nikolai. The one beside Elena had her eyes—a relative, he assumed. The other standing beside Nikolai was roughly the same age as Nagregor, his dark hair gelled down, his eyes cold and hard. His hand rested on Nikolai's shoulder while they all smiled happily into the camera. He felt a pang of sympathy for Elena. She clearly loved the man very much and must have been devastated when he died.

He was replacing the photo when Elena returned carrying a bowl of steaming hot water and some gauze and a white bandage.

"Nikolai," she said simply when she saw the photo he'd been looking at.

He nodded as she sat down at the round dining table. He took the seat beside her. Elena gingerly lifted his hand and gently started cleaning it.

It stung like a son-of-a-bitch, and to take his mind off the pain he started talking. "Who's the other man, the one beside Nikolai?"

"Nikolai's best man, Alexei Dimitrovich, another agent. They were great friends."

Lucas was starting to get used to the pain. He watched her beautiful face as she kept her head bowed, concentrating completely on his wound.

"How long were you married?"

"Three years. He was my supervisor straight out of the academy."

"Earlier you said he was killed but it was more than that, wasn't it? Killed could mean a car accident. But what you meant was that he was murdered?" he asked gently, already knowing the answer. He wanted to keep the discussion open, though he immediately regretted the words when her hand tightened on his. He was about to apologize when she spoke.

"Yes, he was murdered. I was working late one night, and when I came home Nikolai was lying in a pool of his own blood. The place had been ransacked. The official statement was a robbery interrupted."

He caught something in her tone. "But you don't believe that?"

Elena shook her head. "Let's just say red flags went up. Nikolai was a trained SVR agent, and to be taken by a common burglar? No. I don't believe that."

"Signs of struggle?"

Elena shrugged. "They thought so."

He studied her face as she cleaned his wound. "Who is they?"

"The investigators. It was too organized, you know...random chaos. It took me days to sort through the mess. Nothing was taken, at least nothing I could determine."

Lucas followed her gaze, though he wondered if they were seeing the same things. He imagined she was in the past, seeing the room in disarray. Nikolai was murdered here, he surmised. In this very apartment. He shivered as a chill shot down his back.

"Do you have the report they made?" he asked.

She nodded.

"Can I see it?"

She frowned, obviously trying to decide why he wanted it. Finally she gave up and went to the writing desk nearby and opened the drawer. She shifted through some files before pulling one out and handing it to him. He assumed the Russian letters on the front read *Nikolai Nagregor*.

He opened the manila folder and took a second to glance at the information before moving on. Elena had found him. The thought sickened him as he saw the color photographs of her husband lying on the floor. He could only imagine what finding a loved one like that would do to a person. He immediately admired the woman for continuing with her life. She was tough. He admired her all the more. It couldn't have been easy. He took in what Elena had called 'random chaos' and she was right. The apartment hadn't been burglarized but it certainly had been tossed. Someone had been looking for something in particular. He doubted they found whatever it was. Nikolai was by all accounts a great agent. There was no way in hell he left something worth his life out in the open for anyone to find.

"You're right. I think they were looking for something. You know, Pochenchov said Nagregor found a mole inside Russian Intelligence."

Elena's head jerked up from looking at his hand. She pinned him with her cool gaze. "You asked about Nikolai?"

Lucas nodded. "Yes. I had a hunch. I'm not much into coincidence and Nikolai's murder just didn't sit right. I believe he learned something that someone wanted to keep secret."

Elena mulled that over. "Did Pochenchov say who?"

He fell into those grey depths, losing himself for a moment before moving his attention back to the conversation.

"No. But I'm going to find the son-of-a-bitch. He has a lot to answer for. I just have to lay low for a while."

Elena wrapped the white bandage around his palm. He could tell she had done this before. The bandage was tight enough to stop the bleeding and keep the wound clean but loose enough that he didn't lose any feeling in his fingers. With a husband like Nikolai, he assumed he would have taught her how to correctly clean and bandage wounds.

What would it be like to have a woman like Elena? Nikolai had been one lucky S-O-B. He hoped the man knew that and had appreciated his wife. There was a lot to appreciate. She was unlike any woman he had ever met. It was just his luck she lived on a different continent and had already given her heart to another. He had a feeling if there was ever a woman to tie him down, it would be Elena. He had a sense she would complement him and his pursuits, rather than hinder him. She seemed to understand his choices and had supported her husband's career. But then, even if she could move on from Nikolai, would she risk her heart again to a man who constantly put his life in danger? He doubted it. It was a nice fantasy but one that would never come true.

Elena stood and started gathering up the used cloth. Lucas looked up from admiring her handywork.

"You're really good at that. Thanks."

Elena nodded, her lips pressed into a tight line. He caught hold of her wrist, effectively stopping her from moving away.

"Elena, what is it?"

She sat heavily in her chair, her face burdened with guilt and apology. "I can't help you. It's not that I don't want to," she quickly added. "I wish I could, but I have no standing with SVR. I was only reinstated to active status yesterday so I could work your case."

"Why?"

She frowned. "Because no one else wanted the job."

Lucas shook his head. She was either evasive or hadn't understood what he was asking. He was hoping for the latter. He didn't like thinking she was lying to him or purposely being ambiguous. He acknowledged the unreasonable thought. He barely knew her and she had no loyalty to him. It was stupid to think she owed him any. But still, he would like to think she was being honest with him.

"No, I meant why were you on probation?"

She sighed audibly. "Nikolai. I wouldn't leave it alone. I challenged the investigator's ruling. Caused insurmountable problems. I was deemed too emotional and placed on desk duty."

Lucas heard heavy footsteps stop outside her door, followed by a large fist knocking.

A man's voice came at them through the door, his Russian thick, his voice gravelly. "Elena Ivanova? Please open the door!"

"*Govno*," Elena cussed, jumping up from her seat. Lucas didn't have to know the language to recognize the four letter expletive.

Her face morphed into one of horror and whispered, "SVR."

"Fuck." No time for niceties, he needed to get out of there now. "Look, do you want to find out what happened to Nikolai?"

Elena's eyes widened. "Of course I do."

"Then we'll have to make a break for it."

Elena gave him an 'are you kidding?' look. He knew what she was thinking. They were two floors up, and that wasn't the only obstacle in their way.

The SVR agent began pounding on the door, repeating his warning. Lucas was quickly running out of time.

"Are you serious? I could lose my job if I ally myself with a wanted man. Not to mention that Russians don't exactly have a good reputation for treating traitors well."

He understood her position and concern. She was stuck between a rock and a hard place and he felt like an ass asking her for help. He knew he was desperate enough to play the Nikolai card. "We know someone is playing on both sides within the government."

Elena nodded, her furtive gaze going from her door then back to him. "A tip from a known weapons dealer won't stand. And not to mention you don't have a name or even a suspect."

Lucas was beyond desperate. There was no one else who could help him. He was alone in a foreign country, a wanted man, and didn't speak the language. He was far from home and in a shit load of trouble. It would take Jim weeks to get him out alive if he even survived the day, which at the moment wasn't looking too promising.

"Elena, please," he implored. "I can't do this myself. I need your help."

Her brow furrowed and a look of surrender passed over her face.

"*Sraka*," she muttered under breath. He didn't think he wanted to know what that meant and didn't ask. He had a feeling it was about him. He gave her a huge grin, and her eyes narrowed. He certainly wasn't as charming as he thought or she was just immune to his gift.

Lucas grabbed her arm and dragged her over to the window overlooking the street. Elena only had time to snatch up her purse from where she had dumped it earlier before he was pulling her with him across the room.

He heard the agent trying to break in. The door shuddered as the man's shoulder connected with wood. He opened the window and gave a cursory look out before turning to Elena.

"Brace yourself!"

Elena's eyes widened. "Are you serious?" she demanded.

He gave another look out the window and shrugged. "Don't worry. I'm sure the snow will break your fall."

I hope.

"Or a leg," Elena stated.

Yeah, or a leg. She didn't need to make it sound like this was something he *wanted* to do. They had no other choice. He didn't fancy spending twenty to thirty in a Russian prison freezing his balls off.

Elena hiked up her skirt until it reached the tops of her thighs, just long enough to keep her modesty, and climbed through the window onto the small ledge outside. He joined her shortly after.

"Ready on three, one…"

The sound of snapping wood reverberated throughout the apartment. The SVR agent stumbled inside. Within seconds, two more agents followed with their guns drawn. They certainly don't mess around here. He wondered at what it would take to provoke them into shooting. Probably not a lot.

Elena grabbed his hand. "Three."

She jumped, taking him with her, both landing on their backs in the snow. Lucas was on his feet in seconds while Elena tested the mobility of her appendages. Taking her hands in his, he deftly pulled her to her feet. He kept hold of one of her hands and started dragging her down the street before she could protest. He could see more SVR vehicles approaching in the distance. As they drew near, he yanked Elena into a nearby alley and pushed her behind a dumpster, following closely. He watched as the cars drove past and let out a deep breath. One crisis averted. He felt Elena shivering beside him and for the first time, noticed she wasn't wearing a coat.

Shit, he hadn't thought of that when he decided to jump out the window. With this temperature, she would be frozen within the hour. He took off his coat and handed it to her, but she shook her head. He grabbed her arm and roughly shoved it through the sleeve hole. She relented and worked her arm through the other one before buttoning the coat up, giving him a grateful look.

They had to get off the street and into a safe place, wherever that might be. He took Elena's hand again and together they joined the other people on the busy street.

Chapter 12

Vladimir sat at his desk and listened to the report his men issued him. Elena Ivanova had resisted SVR's efforts to seize the American Special Agent. It was still unclear whether she was a willing participant or if Special Agent Gates had taken her against her will, threatening her with bodily harm and fleeing into the streets. His men were currently searching for them now.

They had to bring Lucas Gates in. He killed one of their own, accidentally or not, and his men would be after blood. It would be quite difficult to bring him in alive. His men were not known for their pleasant treatment of cop killers. As for Elena, she made her decision the moment she went out the window with Gates.

He shouldn't have put her back on the job so quickly. She hadn't been ready. But liaising with the American Special Agent was a job no one had wanted. In a ditch effort to appease the US Government, he'd decided to bring her back into the daily grind. He'd thought she'd follow protocol but he should've expected insubordination. It wasn't the first time she'd rebelled. She had not accepted the report given to her and had gone off the deep end, shouting conspiracy. She had to get it through her thick head that Nikolai's death was just plain bad luck. Although he had to admit he had a tough time swallowing that as well. But he was not one to question. More than likely it was another government's agent who'd had it out for Nagregor, or he just got caught up in the crossfire.

After Nagregor's death, Elena had been interviewed in standard formality to determine what she knew about her husband's job. What secrets did she know that could put her or her country at risk? The agency had been relieved to find Nagregor had kept to the regulations, non-disclosure to spouses or relatives. He had not usually been one to follow the rules, only when they suited him, but he had known the risks. Now his widow was in deep trouble. There would be no getting her out of this unscathed, at least not until they knew the score.

Gates's boss had emphatically denied any wrong doing on his agent's behalf. James Fitzgibbon had told him if Lucas shot an SVR agent, he had a damn good reason for doing so. He had known Lucas for a decade now, knew the type of man he was, and he wasn't the kind to go rogue. He was a dedicated agent of the CIA and loved his country. He wouldn't piss it all away by popping off another agent. Vladimir wasn't concerned about the why. He just wanted to get the mess cleaned up and kept quiet. He gave the order. Bring in Lucas Gates under any circumstances. Pity the person caught in the middle.

Elena, Elena. You should have gotten out while you could.

Soon there would be nowhere safe for Elena Ivanova and Lucas Gates.

Chapter 13

After walking in silence for five minutes, Lucas caught sight of a café and steered Elena towards it. He could feel the warmth radiating from the building and was already imagining a hot beverage flowing down his throat and warming his belly. He opened the door to the café for Elena and she stepped inside, finding her way to an empty booth. When she sat down, his winter coat almost swallowed her whole. She stood back up and removed the coat, placing it beside another coat hanging over the seats of their booth and the adjoining booth occupied by a young couple.

Lucas realized just how cold he was as the heat in the room caused his limbs to thaw out, giving him acute pain. He tried to keep his face impassive, not wanting to concern Elena even more in their current predicament. He rubbed his hands together, grateful when the feeling slowly returned.

A tired looking waitress came up to them, a weary half smile plastered on her face. She looked first at him and then at Elena before speaking in

Russian.

Elena replied in the same language. She glanced at Lucas and asked in English, "Cream or sugar with your coffee?"

"Neither," he answered. Elena then proceeded to relay the information to the waitress who then wandered off to get their coffees.

They sat in silence. Lucas wondered what the hell they were going to do. By asking Elena to help him, he had made her an accomplice. She would be wanted by the very people she worked with. All resources she might have had at her disposal were now gone. Whatever happened, he would make it up to her. Somehow he would right the wrongs he caused and make sure she didn't suffer because she was the unfortunate one to have been handed the job of being a liaison to him. He would also find out the truth of Nikolai's death while he was at it.

He owed her that much at least.

He thought about Nikolai and about his case. They were all connected. He just didn't know how. Six months ago, Nagregor had been assassinated. Pochenchov all but admitted to that, and Lucas knew without doubt the assassin was a professional. Even if he was stone cold drunk, Nikolai wouldn't have let a punk ass burglar get the jump on him. It took a professional to get rid of a professional. Now that thought stunk to high heaven.

"Who do you think Nikolai would've trusted enough to discuss the possibility of a mole inside Russian Intelligence, someone using their status within the agency for illegal activity?"

Elena shrugged. "Depends."

"On?" he encouraged when she didn't speak. He could see her mind working rapidly. He wondered what she was thinking.

"On how far he thought it went up the ladder."

The waitress set down the mugs of steaming coffee and walked away. He and Elena gratefully sipped at their drinks. The hot liquid warmed his body right down to his toes. He almost moaned out loud in delight, catching himself at the last second.

Lucas gave it some thought. "As far as Director Mishkin?"

Elena shook her head. "No, I wouldn't accuse Vladimir without supporting evidence. He might be an arrogant ass but I don't doubt he's a patriot."

"And Nikolai never spoke to you about the possibility of a traitor? Didn't allude to it in any way even hypothetically?"

"No, we never spoke of work. It was prohibited. Even between spouses. Nikolai rarely obeyed the rules, but in that case he did…to protect me. He feared what would happen to me." Her gaze settled over his shoulder. She froze, her eyes large in her pale face. "Oh no," she whispered.

"What?"

Elena motioned behind him. "Look."

Lucas followed her line of sight to a small TV mounted to the wall behind the counter. A morning talk show was absently playing on screen. He swore softly as he caught sight of the breaking news bulletin right before his and Elena's photos were plastered behind the news anchor. His from his passport and hers from her official SVR photo ID.

Oh, fuck.

He was expecting eventually the agency would splash their photos everywhere, but he hadn't expected it to be so soon. Either someone was very efficient in getting his passport photo or they had it lying around. The thought made him pause. Who had it, and why did they have his photo? Were they expecting this? Did they plan it? Was this a contingency plan? Questions caused his head to pound.

He stood up. "We'd better get out of here."

Elena nodded, dropping some bills on the table and turned to retrieve his coat. Together they walked out of the café. The young couple in the booth beside them paid their bill, deciding it was time to move on. They stood up, the woman reaching out for her coat, only to discover it was gone.

Chapter 14

Elena closed and buttoned up her new coat. She hadn't liked stealing the woman's snug winter jacket, but it had been necessary. At least the woman could get herself another. Elena couldn't at the moment. She was now officially on the run. Guilt ate at her, but she pushed it aside. Now was not a time for conscience.

She didn't blame SVR for putting out the bulletin. She had aligned herself with Lucas and in their eyes against the agency. She was going to find it difficult to explain her actions when this was all over, if she even got that chance. Right after she and Lucas found out what the hell was going on.

Lucas hadn't seemed to mind her thievery. In fact, he looked amused. She guessed he was a 'when the chips are down, every man for himself' kind of guy. He walked over to a light blue Chevrolet parked at the curb and retrieved what appeared to be a cell phone from his pocket. He pointed the antenna at the vehicle and she watched, speechless, as the indicator lights flashed and the central locking was disabled. The engine automatically started.

She shook her head. *Boys and their toys*. Lucas walked over to the driver's side and opened the door. She had half expected the alarm to go off, catching them in the act.

"We're going to add grand theft auto to our crime spree?" she asked sweetly.

Lucas's eyes twinkled with mischief, a grin on his face that had her heart thumping in her chest. "Well, yeah, unless you want to walk all day?" His expression told her he was not looking forward to it.

Elena let out a deep sigh. "I thought only James Bond had gadgets like that," she told him as she opened the passenger's side door.

Lucas winked at her over the hood. "The agency has nothing on Q."

"Glad to hear that," she replied, relieved. All the world needed was for the Americans to be walking around with that kind of spy arsenal. Although she shuddered to think what was being cooked up in the basement of Langley.

"And I never leave home without it," he said as he pocketed the device.

Screeching tires had them both turning. Two SVR GMC Terrain SUV vehicles were bearing down on them.

"Get in the car!"

Elena didn't wait to be asked twice. She scrambled into the car and was in the process of closing her door when Lucas pulled away from the curb and merged with the other motorists on the busy street, exceeding the speed limit as he tried to put some distance between them and their pursuers.

She glanced behind and saw the chase was on. Another shiny black GMC Terrain SUV had joined the other two.

"Another one," she informed Lucas.

"I see it." He navigated a sharp turn without slowing. He must have had a high speed chase maneuvering lesson at some point, because he handled the car as well as any NASCAR driver she'd seen on TV. She watched the scenery blur outside the window as Lucas weaved in and out of traffic, sometimes bringing their car up on the footpath. Her head hit the ceiling as they ascended and descended rapidly as they passed over a speed bump and she let out an *oomph*.

The Terrain wasn't far behind them. They didn't even bother to slow down as they sideswiped an unsuspecting motorist. She shivered as she thought what might happen should they catch them. She hoped Lucas was as good as he appeared to be. She didn't fancy spending the best years of her life in prison.

She stared out the window as she willed her heart to slow down, watching some of Moscow's beautiful sights, the triumphal arch on Kutuzov Avenue, Ostankino Tower, and the Novodevichy Convent pass by, and realized she wished she could share her country's landmarks with Lucas. She was extremely proud to be Russian, a true patriot. *Perhaps another time*, she thought as she was jerked into his shoulder as he took another corner too fast.

Pop. Pop.

She frowned at the strange sound and looked back at the vehicles in pursuit.

"Oh my God, are they *shooting* at us?" she asked him, incredulous.

He spared a glance at the rear view mirror.

"Seems that way to me," he replied, unfazed.

He didn't seem surprised or concerned, which frustrated the hell out of her. He could at least act scared. She, however, didn't have to act. She was frightened and getting shot at was not helping the situation. "And you're not worried about that?"

He shrugged. "The possibility of them actually making a direct hit is extremely limited with the vehicle traveling at the speed ours is."

She heard more popping and then the sound of metal hitting metal as a bullet connected with the undercarriage of the Chevrolet. Lucas swerved to accommodate the impact.

"You were saying?"

He shrugged again. "It's not an exact science."

Staring into the side mirror, she watched in horror as her fellow SVR agents leaned out their car windows, their guns aimed in her direction, trying to shoot out their tires. She worried for the bystanders, afraid one of them might be hit. Lucas navigated the car in and out of the thickening morning traffic, through red lights and up onto a curb narrowly missing a street light. Nervous sweat coated her skin. She hoped she didn't die today. It was an uncertainty but in the back of her mind, she trusted Lucas's driving skills. She heard a loud thump and the sickening sound of a car's chassis compress. She glanced behind them. One of the

GMC Terrain's following them had not been so lucky to miss the street light, parking the SUV dead center, the hood crumpled at the force of the smash.

As they went through another red light, she held on tight to the handle above the door. Her left hand held the edge of her seat in a death grip. She glanced over at Lucas, who wore an expression of deep concentration. Perspiration coated his forehead at the exertion required to keep from losing control of the car. His long fingers gripped the steering wheel hard. She heard another sound of metal folding and glanced back to see another SVR issued vehicle crash as a disgruntled driver smashed into the vehicle while trying to go through the intersection. The driver got out and started swearing a blue streak. His attitude would soon change when he found out who was driving the other car.

She let out a sigh of relief as there was only one more SUV in pursuit. She closed her eyes and tried for deep, calming breaths. She was not one for this kind of excitement and had never longed for adventure. She was quite content with her life as it was. She liked knowing what to expect and this was certainly not on her list.

"Buckle up," Lucas advised.

She saw where he was headed and muttered another curse, vaguely surprised at her herself. Not one to swear often, she had definitely tripled her quota since meeting him. She quickly buckled herself in then reached across his lap to do the same for him as he pulled out of traffic, going down a set of pedestrian stairs to the street below. They bounced up and down as the tires connected with the uneven ground.

The SUV behind them followed suit. Lucas pressed down harder on the accelerator as they practically flew down the steps, the tires now barely touching the ground. They hit the street below hard, sliding across the asphalt as Lucas fought to correct it. Trying to lose their tail, he steered the vehicle across the lanes of incoming traffic and turned right to drive down along a street adjacent to Alexander Gardens, past a Metro station and café. It was a tight fit and Lucas expertly squeezed through, narrowly avoiding hitting a row of tightly parked cars.

Elena resisted the urge to close her eyes, needing to see what came next in order to prepare herself. The cars beside them blurred as they sped past. If her window had been down, she could have reached out and touched them. She could see the busy intersection up ahead. She turned to the back window. Behind them, the black GMC was once more gaining on them.

The Chevrolet protested the speed at which Lucas executed a hard left at the end of the street, going around the sharp turn on two wheels amidst squealing tires and burning rubber. He never once eased off the accelerator, immediately correcting the steering wheel as he brought them into another tight alley. He spun the wheel quickly, just managing to avoid plowing into a dumpster.

She fought the urge to gulp, grabbing hold of the hand brace above her door with one hand while the other one pressed hard against the glove box in an attempt to keep from smacking into the dashboard.

Were these guys ever going to give up? The Government vehicle followed them down the street, gaining on them at an alarming rate. An admirable trait unless you were the one under pursuit. She glanced over at Lucas who kept his eyes firmly on the road. There wasn't a lot of wiggle room and they couldn't afford to crash. She refused to think about what would happen to them if they did.

Pop. Pop.

Elena couldn't hold back the squeal that escaped. What the hell was going on? Nothing Lucas had done in the past twenty-four warranted such a reaction and it made her wonder what he may have stumbled upon.

Pop. Pop.

She felt the back tire deflate. Someone had gotten in a lucky shot. She watched as Lucas fought to control the car as they drove along a stretch of road between the Kremlin and the Moska River. The SVR tail came up behind, undaunted by the narrowness of the street, pushing their speed higher in an attempt to catch up with them.

The black Terrain—finally having gained on them due to difficulties Lucas experienced with the flat tire, unable to push the vehicle faster—clipped the tail of the Chevrolet causing it to spin around a few times, hitting the larger SUV as it did so. The force of the impact caused the Terrain to flip over before eventually ramming the Chevrolet's right side into the wall of a nearby structure.

Elena felt like she was going to throw up. Her head spun and her heart thumped in her throat. Her whole body ached from the jostle it had received.

Lucas turned to face her, surveying her for any damage. He seemed relieved so she assumed she wasn't bleeding or dying.

"Elena? Are you all right?" he asked, concern clear in his voice. He reached over and released her seatbelt before pushing a loose strand that had escaped her chignon from her face.

She caught her breath. "Do all Americans drive like that?"

Lucas grinned. "Only the good ones."

He got out of the car and waited for her to shimmy over from the passenger side and exit through the driver's door since her side was wedged against a wall. She was thankful for the stretchy fabric of her skirt as she inelegantly climbed out of the car. Just then she heard the sound of material ripping and sighed. Apparently it wasn't *that* stretchy.

Her knees almost buckled under her weight. Lucas caught her about the waist and held her upright for a second while she gained her legs before taking her hand in his. They began to move quickly away from the scene of the accident.

"Hope he had insurance," Lucas added as an afterthought.

Elena narrowed her eyes at him. "You're making jokes at a time like this?" she scolded. Her heart rate had yet to return to normal and the adrenaline was pumping heavily through her veins.

He gave her a brief look. "Would you prefer sarcasm?"

She shook her head and told herself she wouldn't smile. She would *not* encourage such outrageous behavior. How could he stand there and pretend the last hour did not just happen? She had never been more scared in her entire life. She could feel the hysteria welling up inside her and resisted the urge to hit him. Hard.

"I would prefer good ideas," she said instead. "Less John Wayne antics and more Isaac Newton revelations."

"I'll try to be accommodating," he said dryly.

The tires of a car squealing behind them caught their attention and they both turned around. Another SVR vehicle was coming at them. *Not again*. She couldn't take much more of this. Lucas yanked her hand and they took off running, only just avoiding being hit by the Terrain as it sped towards them.

Elena was grateful for the tear in her skirt as it allowed her to keep pace with Lucas's fast, long strides, something she was sure she wouldn't have been able to accomplish had it not torn. She took the lead, this time pulling on Lucas's hand, directing him into the throng of people congregating in nearby Red Square, in hopes of losing themselves in the crowd. She squished through the mass of tourists across the center of the square, running past the multi-colored domes of St. Basil's Cathedral.

They made it to the opposite side of the square, dipping into a small, obscure alleyway. They looked out onto Red Square, checking for signs of their pursuers. There were none. They had finally lost them. Relief filled her body and made her feel almost euphoric.

Still catching her breath she said, "It appears they have given up for now."

Lucas nodded. They stayed in the alley for a while longer. Her mind refused to be silent. They couldn't stay out in the cold all day. She and Lucas would need to go someplace warm. The temperature had already dropped her body warmth and she could feel the cold chilling her. The exertion and subsequence perspiration was not helping to keep her body heat in.

"Are you all right?" he asked.

Her eyes misted. She was shaking and could feel the tears threatening to spill. She tried desperately to blink them back. She knew she couldn't trust her voice so instead she nodded.

"Hey," he said softly and moved closer to her. "It's all right."

He pulled her into his chest, wrapping his strong arms around her. She melted into him, allowing herself to lean on him for just a moment. It had been a chaotic morning following an emotional six months and was proving to be too much. But in that moment she didn't feel so alone.

"I'm fine," she said and then the floodgates opened. The tears she had gallantly fought back now trickled down her cheeks. Her ungloved fingers scrunched up his coat as she tightened her fist around the fabric on his sleeve. Her other hand rested on his solid chest.

Sobs racked her body, but barely any sound came out her mouth which was currently pressed hard against his shoulder. His hands rubbed up and down her back in unconscious movement as a way to give her comfort and she was thankful for such kindness. Despite how weak it made her appear.

He pulled her closer, almost as if he planned to never let her go and she was more than happy to go along with him wherever he went. She pulled strength from him and instantly felt better, more in control.

She sniffled, her hand wiping at her face. "I'm okay now."

She pulled back some but still remained in the comfort of his arms. She missed this connection to another person and was enjoying it far more than she should.

"You sure?" he asked, concern in his voice again.

She nodded, feeling like an idiot. Now was not the time or place for mental breakdowns. One good thing came of it, though. Having Lucas's arms around her had felt wonderful. Oddly, it had felt right. Almost familiar in a way. Her body had molded to his as if it had always belonged there. It had been a long time since she had been held. There had been the occasional awkward shoulder pat but never the bear-like hug Lucas had given her and was still currently giving her. His body was muscular and powerful beneath her hands and against her chest. Strong. Comforting. She never wanted him to let her go.

Had she imagined him kissing her head?

She inhaled his scent, the pheromones radiating from him, causing her head to spin and her body to warm. She recognized it as desire. She wanted to wrap her arms around him and hold on forever. She wanted him. Her mind was a riot of thoughts, none helpful at the moment. His mesmerizing blue gaze caught hers and her heart started pounding painfully in her chest, this time not caused by fear, and her breath caught in her throat. She couldn't get over the damage that man caused her senses. She stepped back out of his delicious arms before she did something stupid. Like kiss him. Or worse.

She instantly felt cold and alone and fought her weak body into giving up and returning once more to his embrace. Why now?

Because now was certainly not the time or place. They were on the run, chased by her own government, her own agency. Now was definitely not a good time to be getting aroused. They had things to do and a traitor to catch.

Lucas frowned as she put space between them. She looked out at the square as she ran her hands up and down her arms, trying to warm her body.

"So do you have a plan yet?" she asked, her voice quivering. She turned and faced him as he moved closer to her. She could feel the heat from his body closing in around her.

"Besides escaping capture?" he shrugged. "Not really, something along the lines of finding out what the fuck is going on."

She nodded.

"I don't like where all this is heading. Michael Ducane is here, he met with Alvin Pochenchov, and now he's dead. I can't swallow that coincidence. It all seems so final."

She thought about that. Alvin Pochenchov had a lot of enemies. But if a lone SVR agent shot him, something was going on beneath the surface. There could only be one reason for taking a well-connected weapons dealer like Pochenchov out of the picture.

"They're tying up loose ends."

The question was, what did Ducane need and why? What was he going to do with supplies he had purchased from Pochenchov? Lucas took her hand in his. She read concern and something else in his eyes. Something she couldn't identify. "I'm sorry I got you involved in this."

She made a dismissing motion with her free hand. "Don't. I'm glad you did."

He gave her a disbelieving look.

"Really," she continued. "I know it didn't seem like it in the beginning, but if there is something wrong deep inside SVR, I want to find out what that is. Especially if it explains why Nikolai is dead. I'm sorry I cried all over your coat."

He smiled at her and caressed her cheek with his thumb. "I'm not. You're only human, Elena. Besides, I like being the knight in shining armor."

"Yes, well, you may think you're a knight but I feel silly and embarrassed."

He leaned closer to her, their lips inches apart. She stopped breathing. "I'll make you a deal. We get through this and I'll let you be there the next time I make a fool of myself. It shouldn't take long. I tend to live with my foot in my mouth."

At the word 'mouth' her eyes went to his lips, pale from the cold. She swallowed hard and quickly looked away.

"I'll hold you to that," she said softly.

Chapter 15

Lucas tightened his hand around Elena's as he looked out at the people blissfully ignorant of what went on around the world. What he would give to be one of the tourists out in the square, happily snapping pictures for their holiday album. He had a thought.

"Well, now that our faces are being broadcast across Russia, we'll have to change our looks."

Elena nodded at the same time she shivered. He pulled her closer to him. She went willingly and a surge of satisfaction shot through him. "And we have to get out of the cold," Elena said. "It's supposed to be a record low today."

Fantastic, just what we needed.

He took off his scarf and tucked Elena's silky hair up under the wool before wrapping the scarf around her neck. She was somewhat disguised. At least she wouldn't be recognized easily.

"Gorgeous," he said when he was done and gave her a wink.

"What about you? You stick out like a sore

thumb."

She patted down his blond hair.

He grinned at her. "Yeah, well, unless you have any ideas?"

She thought about it for a moment, her face lighting up. "I may have one."

She led him out of the alley, mingling with the tourists as they headed for a small Orthodox Chapel standing almost hidden to the side. Next to the entrance was a stall peddling tourist souvenirs. Elena stopped and began searching the mass of gaudy trinkets and found what she was after, a traditional Russian grey fur hat. She purchased it, then turned to Lucas and placed it on his head, effectively covering his hair.

"Now you won't be so noticeable."

"Yeah? You think I could pass for one of your countrymen?"

She gave him a long considering look before answering. "If you keep your mouth shut."

As if it was the most natural thing to do, Elena captured his hand in hers and began walking again. He fell into step with her. Looking as if they had all the time in the world, Elena acted as a tour guide as they idly made their way down Red Square, toward the north end away from St. Basil's.

She was calmer now, almost serene. He'd recognized the signs of adrenaline crashing earlier and was thankful he'd managed to soothe her—not that it had been a particularly difficult chore. He found he liked having Elena in his arms.

She spoke and drew his attention back to the present. She pointed to the left and he followed her finger to look at the Kremlin wall. Behind it he could see the Senate Buildings and the Senate Tower that had been built into the wall directly behind Lenin's tomb. Next to the Senate Tower was St. Nicholas Tower. Straight ahead, where Elena was leading him, was the State Historical Museum. The structure was a large turreted crimson building with intricate paneling. "Built on orders of Peter the Great," she told him before pointing out Resurrection Gate to the right of the museum.

She was proud of her heritage and let it show as she talked, her eyes alight. She had a lot to be proud of, he reflected as he took in the amazing sights. He'd never been interested in history, but Elena's passion was quickly changing that.

"We'll stop in here and warm ourselves," Elena told him. "Museum patrons barely have time or inclination to sit down and watch the news bulletins."

"Really?"

Elena nodded. "I have a friend who works for a museum. She wouldn't know if a man landed on Mars unless he was carrying a rocket full of antiques with him."

Lucas chuckled as they entered, Elena paying the admission fare, retrieving the Russian Rubles from her purse.

He was immediately enveloped by the heat inside the museum. Lucas shivered as it began to warm him from head to toe. He and Elena made a slow tour of the treasures the museum had to offer, taking their time looking at a wide range of garments, weaponry, and manuscripts dating back to the twelfth century.

His mind never stopped, continually thinking through the past twenty-four hours, trying to make sense of the jumble of facts bouncing around his head, wondering where they all fit in. He knew he was missing a huge piece but he just couldn't work out what that may be.

They finished up their tour of the museum on the second floor where a restaurant with delightful hot coffee awaited them.

It was now well past two o'clock in the afternoon, and soon it would be dark. The sun set early in the winter months, which was good for them. At least they would be able to get around much easier under the cover of darkness.

Elena flopped down in a seat at a table in an obscure corner, away from the other patrons and out of earshot from anyone who might listen in. He could see she was exhausted, having been up for over twenty-four hours, including being shot at and running for her life. Her adrenaline levels had plummeted fast and would've wiped out her energy reserves. She was going to crash and soon. He didn't want to have to push her any farther. He wished he could just let her rest.

She hadn't once complained. She had been a downright trouper through the entire affair. It couldn't be easy on her. She barely knew him. Didn't know the kind of person he was. He would have to ask her one day why she put her trust in him. But now wasn't the time. He was already having trouble maintaining his distance. Holding her had been complete torture. He'd wanted to comfort her, yet all he could think of was how he wanted to know what her body felt like. It had done nothing but tease him mercilessly, making him wonder what it would be like to touch her without the layers of clothes and heavy winter coats.

But there was something more than just physical attraction. He cared for her. His heart hurt knowing he'd pushed her to breaking point and he wanted to take away all her pain. He'd pressed a light kiss into her hair before he could stop himself and wished he'd never gone to her apartment for help. He had brought her into this dangerous situation and had no idea how to get her out again. This was her country and their rules. There was no help for them. They were alone.

At least we're together.

The thought popped into his mind and he was thankful she was with him no matter the circumstance. She was the rainbow in the overcast sky, the one good thing to come out of this entire mess. He hadn't known her long but knew he could trust her.

Elena ordered two coffees and something hot to eat. He was immensely grateful for as soon as she'd mentioned food, his stomach growled and demanded sustenance. They waited until their food arrived and the waitress left before getting back to discussing their dilemma.

It would help if they had a place to start. He supposed he should start back with Nikolai Nagregor since that was where it all seemed to originate—with his death. He needed to find a way to read the police report in English, see if there was something the investigators missed. All of which would be difficult to get hold of since both he and Elena were now on every watch list the country had.

"We're running around Moscow wanted, hunted, and unarmed. We aren't going to last long," Elena said matter-of-factly.

Lucas nodded, already aware of the harsh truth. A thought popped into his head. One he knew she wasn't going to like. "Then we will go where even the SVR have no jurisdiction. Well, at least none that will be paid attention to."

Puzzled, she asked, "And where's that?"

"The friendly neighborhood mob," he replied.

"Do all Americans have a death wish or is it just you?"

Chapter 16

He listened as President Sergei Smirnov of the Russian Federation spoke. The microphone before him sent his voice to the far reaches of the room. He could barely conceal his hatred of the man. He had shown little promise from the start, but now he was a complete disappointment. He had not voted for the man in the last election, preferring his rival, Yuri Volstov's political policy over Smirnov's. He had long since lost his respect for his president when the man had announced the previous year his plan to back all of the United States endeavors, that together they would fight anyone who sought to do the world harm.

He couldn't believe it. The man had no backbone. Following all the others into pooling Russia's little resources together in an effort to support the United States in wars of their own making. Russia was the superior nation. When would his beloved country finally be recognized as such? *Certainly not while a man like Smirnov is in charge, that's for he sure*, he thought savagely. The man was useless, nothing but a mongrel dog waiting to be fed the scraps from the American president's dinner table. Disgusting.

His body tensed and he tried to control the rage inside him. His blood boiled and his hand curled into a fist. They had been the first into space, beating the arrogant Americans by a decade, and yet all the world bloody remembered were the names Armstrong, Aldrin, and NASA. He took a deep breath, shuddering at the force of will it took not to go right up to Smirnov and rip his goddamned head off.

It will all be over soon.

Soon, he would no longer have to stand here and listen to the shit coming out of the imposter's mouth. Sergei Smirnov would die and he would watch. He nodded to a fellow agent as they escorted the president down from the podium where he had been speaking and past him, through the small door that led to the back of the building where a car was waiting. He spoke into his radio, advising the agents by the vehicle the president was on his way to them.

He looked about the room, as a vigilant agent would, checking the crowd for signs of anarchy. It wouldn't do for the president to be assassinated now. No, he wouldn't allow anyone to mess up his plans. His carefully devised and executed plans. When satisfied no attempt would be made, he turned and followed the president's path through the door. In just a few short hours he would be in St. Petersburg and the countdown would begin.

It was time for a new government, a new order.

He had planned everything down to the smallest

possible detail and until recently it had gone like clockwork. But he was a man to bounce back on his feet, quickly recalculating to allow for the unexpected change to his plan in the guise of a CIA agent. He had not thought the United States to be so prompt in sending one of their own to deal with the situation. But he was nothing if not resilient and had immediately gone about remedying the issue. Luck would have it that the American was so accommodating. It had been child's play to brand him a rogue and set every law enforcement agency in the country on his ass.

He didn't like unforeseen problems, instead priding himself on being able to anticipate every eventuality. He wasn't a stupid man and while he was optimistic, he hadn't climbed as far as he had without learning the key to survival. He wasn't about to be caught and linked to the plot should something go awry and had ensured a contingency plan. He only hoped he didn't have to use it because that meant he had failed. There was no telling when another opportunity would fall into their laps.

It had been a stroke of genius that had him seeking out and securing Ducane's services for the job. Nothing could lead back to him or to Yuri Volstov. It would do no good to have suspicion thrown on the assassinated president's successor, otherwise everything would be for naught.

Ducane was the perfect scapegoat for the aftermath, already having proved himself as the culprit of several other political bombings across the globe. The blame would be placed squarely on his shoulders and Ducane would not be alive to name the man who'd hired him. He would shoot him dead while 'trying' to protect his president. The building, though well-guarded, had several entry points and a man in his high position could easily smuggle in a terrorist and keep the crowd contained while appearing to be doing his very best to get everyone out alive.

Soon the world would know that the weak were falling, and only the strong would survive. And he was very strong, and with his help, his country would be too.

Chapter 17

The cold had settled in for the night, getting to a low of minus five and was still dropping. By morning it would easily be minus ten. Snow had stopped falling and the clouds had locked in the freezing temperature. Still, the bitter climate did not deter everyone from leaving their residences. The nightlife in the neighborhood of Solntsevskaya was well known in Russia for being Moscow's largest Mafiya neighborhood. The Solntsevskaya Bratva— the brotherhood—was one of the most lethal and feared factions and was a far cry from that of Tverskaya Street. Men lay crumpled on the ground long since frozen to death, the smell of bodies, sweat, alcohol, and urine ripe in the frigid air.

Lucas never let his eyes rest, scanning everything and everyone as a threat. He liked to know when he was about to be involved in a royal fuck up.

"Stick close," he murmured to Elena, watching the condensation come from his mouth. He had long since lost feeling in his toes and silently cursed the foul weather. They had spent the entire day at the museum, trying to come up with an appropriate plan of attack, but missing key bits of information put them at a disadvantage, that and the fact they had no bargaining chips. They had finally agreed to see where the night took them.

Elena glanced uneasily about the street. "Yes, because I'll be wandering off any moment now," she replied dryly.

He smiled at the sarcasm in her voice, his smile quickly disappearing as he watched two men with giant guns bulging proudly under their coats approach them.

The left one spouted off quick Russian. Elena tensed beside him.

"I don't think they want us here," she said, her voice soft as if she was afraid that a higher decibel would set them off.

"Even I caught that. Okay, translate for me. I want to speak to your boss. It involves a shipment of his."

Elena frowned. He could clearly see she did not want to be here. Nor did she want to address the man standing in front of her. She most certainly didn't want to relay his message, which she probably assumed—and correctly—would royally piss them off. He had offered for her to stay behind but she wouldn't hear it and refused to be cosseted away. He still felt tingles in his body as she'd told him, in no uncertain terms, "Where you go, I go. We're in this together."

Elena took a deep breath, visibly preparing herself for the confrontation. *Such a trouper*, he thought again. He would really have to do something nice for her when he was done messing up her life and possibly getting her killed in the process.

Elena repeated his message, the man's face darkening. He had not liked what he heard. He raised his hand. Lucas went still, then relaxed when he saw the man bring up a cell phone and press a speed dial button before speaking fast into the phone.

He studied Lucas as he spoke, nodded curtly, and hung up the phone. He turned to Elena and spoke to her. She nodded her response and took hold of Lucas's arm with a firm grip.

"We're to follow him," she said, once again speaking softly.

He glanced at her. She didn't appear any more worried than she had a few moments ago. He leaned down so his mouth was close to her ear and asked, "You didn't happen to overhear any of what was said on the other end did you? Give us an idea of what to expect?"

She shook her head and together they started following the man.

"No, but I didn't catch the words, kill, maim, murder, disappear, or river so I think he's pretty interested in what you have to say." She looked at him. "I must admit, I'm curious too."

He gave her a smile. "Relax, I haven't killed us yet."

He felt some tension leave her body, but she was still pretty stiff. Then again, that could be because of the cold. She returned his smile, albeit slightly smaller. He felt his body respond with a painful tightening and forced his mind back to the danger he had led them both into.

"*Yet* being the operative word, Lucas," she replied.

They followed the man into a shop on the main street. The entrance was off to the side in a concealed alley. *How very gangster of them*, he thought. The building looked like it should have been condemned years ago. It had been once a restaurant and still held some booths and a counter. Dust coated each surface and in places the ceiling plaster had fallen. They walked up a flight of steps and entered another world. The room was richly decorated with a fully stocked bar. Hard wood floors—covered with mink rugs—shined. Long leather couches, a big LCD screen with Dolby Stereos and all the trimmings stood to one side. An elderly man who looked like some child's grandfather sat at a table eating dinner consisting of lobster and caviar. He took a sip of what he could only assume was vodka from the glass in front of him and regarded them coolly.

Marlon Brando he was not. The man's thinning hair was slicked over to one side, his bushy white eyebrows in dire need of a trim, and he wore an expensive suit, seeming tailored just for him.

His black eyes stared right into Lucas's. The man was as cold as ice. He then turned his attention to Elena, his gaze drifting up and down her body. Lucas had the desire to stand in front of her to protect from the old man's sins, and his hands curled into fists, hanging uselessly beside his thighs.

The old man turned his attention back to him and smiled. He knew the effect he had on others and apparently approved of Lucas. He didn't believe that was a good thing.

The man spoke in Russian, his voice gravelly from what Lucas thought had been a pack a day habit.

Elena turned to translate just as the man repeated his question, this time in English. "What about my shipment?"

"First, I need some things from you," Lucas declared.

The old man laughed. Elena's head swung back to face him.

"You're negotiating with the Mafiya?" She sounded incredulous.

Lucas kept his eyes on the Man in Charge. He sensed Elena's fear and anger but couldn't risk addressing them now. He'd rather keep them alive so she could be annoyed with him later.

"I am Iosif Simonov. You are a very brave young man. That or a very stupid one." Iosif smiled. "I could use a man like you. You have quite the set of balls on you."

Elena stiffened beside him. He spared her a quick glance. She was staring at the Russian with unreadable eyes. It was the first time he'd seen her closed off. She was usually an open book and he wondered what caused the transformation.

Iosif continued. "What is it that you want?"

"Guns, good ones," he said.

"I don't have any other kind," Iosif stated truthfully. He wasn't boasting. It was clear he knew the quality of his merchandise and wouldn't have them if they weren't top grade.

"We have a deal then?" Lucas clarified.

Iosif nodded curtly. He was a busy man who didn't have time for games. If he wasn't about to deal, they would be getting fitted for a cement shoe right about now.

"The drug shipment coming in on Tuesday is dirty. One of your men rolled over. You might want a change of location, unless you like hundreds of SVR agents at your party."

Iosif's eyes widened. "And how do you happen to know this?"

Lucas shrugged, folding his arms across his chest, looking nonchalant. "I have myself a spy or two inside Russian Intelligence."

Iosif laughed, wrinkles appearing at the edge of his eyes revealing his age. He stood up. "Follow me."

Lucas took hold of Elena's hand and pulled her close into his body, protecting her. Now would come the true test. He didn't like not knowing his surroundings. If it went belly up, it would be difficult at best to get Elena out of there.

They followed Iosif back down to the restaurant and out the door to a large dark Hummer parked by the building. Iosif shook his head slightly at the two beefy men standing guard at the car, most likely letting them know silently he was not being held by gun point. If Lucas hadn't been looking for such a sign, he would never have seen it.

Iosif barked orders at the two men who promptly snapped into motion. Lucas relied on Elena's response on what was going down. In a way, he felt blind, only having her to guide him through. Trusting her with his life in the dangerous situation they found themselves in. Elena's demeanor didn't change, so he took that as everything was okay. Or the best it could be considering the situation.

Lucas watched as Iosif's men opened the trunk of the car to reveal a large selection of high powered sniper rifles, elite revolvers, and a vast cornucopia of assorted weapons.

Elena's eyes bulged. Lucas felt giddy like a kid in a candy store. He stepped closer and perused the collection, noting the Dragunov Sniper Rifle and an AN-94 Assault Rifle, the latter used by elite Russian Military. He admired the Serbian Zastava M93 Black Arrow Sniper Rifle as he picked up a UK Adams MK4 revolver before replacing it with a Makarov PM eight round pistol. He took stock of the other weapons in the truck of the car. A Desert Eagle and American 180 SMG .22 caliber were also featured. It was a complete shopping list for the everyday criminal.

Iosif smiled proudly. "State of the art weapons. Not even SVR have these," he said.

Lucas nodded. "I've never seen a finer collection."

Iosif's eyes twinkled. "May I ask what you plan on doing with your selection?"

Lucas held the old man's gaze, determined to make his point very clear. "I have no plans to interfere with your family or business. We have a different target in mind."

Iosif accepted his word that he would not use his

weapons against the Bratva. It would be a suicide mission but just maybe Lucas could've been stupid enough to try. Iosif was hardly a man to take chances. That was why he was in charge and still alive. He looked at Elena before turning back to Lucas.

"I would also be willing to make another trade, for your pretty lady here?"

Elena was justly mortified. "I think not!" she blurted out without much thought as to who she was talking to.

"These will do fine, thank you," Lucas said. He thought it best to get Elena the hell out of there, before she said something to offend Iosif. She clearly did not like the man and took little effort to conceal the fact.

"Anytime you want to do business, American, you know where to find me, eh?" He turned to Elena and smiled sweetly. "And you, my dear, are always welcome."

She gave Iosif a smile that was all teeth while one of the men bagged his selections like he was at a supermarket. He almost expected to be asked if he wanted paper or plastic.

What, no receipt?

He took the bag from the Mr. T lookalike with one hand, and with the other grabbed hold of Elena and led her away.

They'd barely made it two streets away when she jerked her arm from his hold. "I can't believe you just traded SVR intel to the Mafiya. That was our only chance to take them down and took years of persuasion and months of planning. Have you any idea what you've just done?"

"Elena, information or money are the only currency men like that deal in. Since we don't have the latter, I had to work with what I had."

She glared at him. "It wasn't yours to give."

She had tears in her eyes and he was instantly contrite. She had a way of making him feel like a pile of shit. It didn't matter he'd done the only thing he could in the moment to get the results he needed, he'd ultimately used her for his own gains. It would be a giant blow to SVR and to the Russian people. He saw that now.

He let out a deep breath. "You're right. It wasn't and I'm sorry. I didn't mean to hurt you and believe me, if there had been any other way...."

He hated that he was still justifying his actions but he wanted her to see there hadn't been another choice. He was a bastard and acknowledging the fact didn't make him feel any better. He was too used to making up the rules as he went and not thinking of the consequences. He should've thought it through and weighed the benefits against the result. He should've taken the time to locate some street vendor selling guns out the back of his car but this had been easiest and now Elena was pissed at him. He studied her face, hoping to see signs of softening, but she remained stoic, the unshed tears glowing as light from the nearby streetlamp washed over her. His heart ached and his arms itched to reach out to hold her as he'd done earlier, but he doubted she would appreciate it now. He wanted her forgiveness more than anything in the world, and the thought he'd so callously hurt her ate away at him.

"I'm sorry," he repeated.

"You don't understand," she said, and walked away from him on unsteady legs.

Chapter 18

Yuri Volstov listened as his challenger spouted off his political views. How the man had gotten elected was beyond him. He was nothing but a conformist. Falling in with the crowd like the sheep he was, following the ideals of others. Their country was a great one and the man was allowing the United States to walk all over him and set the rules they should live by because they thought they know better. He was extremely disappointed at how much of a coward the president was, but he wasn't surprised. Yuri hadn't put much stock in Sergei Smirnov's abilities. The spineless man allowed his countrymen too many liberties. It was time the country took back the power shown to them by their ancestors. Time to show the world who they were, let them not forget who the greater nation was.

When he was sworn in, his first act as president would be to return Russia to its former glory. Some freedoms would need to be sacrificed regrettably, but it was for the greater good. He was sick of sitting on the sidelines watching his beloved country get turned into another America. Soon enough, there would be no law at all and he couldn't—wouldn't—allow that. The problem with the current administration was there were too many people making decisions, the left hand not knowing what the right hand was doing. Only one man could set the laws and that man would be him.

The Soviets had it right the first time. The people might call it a dictatorship, but he called it progression. In today's politics, power, support, and money made the difference. He had many financial backers, others who could see his dream of another golden age of Russia. To make the others think twice before waging wars against them. They would once more be the feared nation. No one would dare cross them. He would succeed where the others had failed. He only had to remove Sergei Smirnov from his seat before he could put his plans into motion.

Then the world had better watch out, because the new Russia—his Russia—would be strong and less forgiving. His Russia would not tolerate interference from those on the outside who would want to change their way of life like the United States had the rest of the world. America was like a plague transforming the world into drones, carbon copies of their failing society. His Russia would allow no such failings. If only Sergei Smirnov was not in power.

He smiled cruelly into the darkness. It was already in motion. His loyal men were out securing his future, their future. Men who used their high positions within their great agencies to further his cause, and he was humble. It was a great honor for so many to put their trust in him, to look to him for leadership, and he would not dare let them down.

Each of his men risked their careers, their very lives every day and stood to be named a traitor should their actions be known. He admired them for their courage, their fortitude, and he would reward all of them in his administration.

He would also pay tribute the fallen, like Igor Zimtovich who had known too much and had to be silenced. Yuri hadn't enjoyed ordering the man's death but Zimtovich had held the smoking gun, the one that would put them all in prison. His intel was what made all of their plans possible. Of course, leaving the body for the Americans to find had been unavoidable and they hadn't anticipated the quick response from the police. It had almost been their downfall, but Yuri's trusted second had taken care of that problem.

And would take care of any other issue that would arise. The man was intelligent and resourceful and had he not shown his devotion to Yuri's cause, Yuri would've been concerned. The man was as blood-thirsty as a vampire and as cold-blooded as any reptile. He himself had witnessed some of his techniques and even now shuddered when he thought of them. He was glad the man was on his side, uniting for a common goal.

Only a select few knew the scope of their takeover, the steps taken to ensure their plan succeeded. It was for their protection as well as his. The fewer who were privy to all, the less loose ends there were to clean up when it was over. Now he would wait while Ducane completed his job and cleared the way for Yuri to become president.

It was a shame so many had to die in his pursuit of supreme and absolute power and domination. Good agents like Nikolai Nagregor who ranked high on the list of men Yuri admired, men who could not be bought or threatened—there were so few of them left. Even men like Pochenchov had their uses, but that was the price. Soon, his Russia would be a power to be reckoned with.

Chapter 19

Once they were well away from Solntsevskaya, Elena stopped and leaned against the closest brick wall. Her legs were unable to hold her vertical any longer. Her heart was still pounding in her chest. She had been up close and personal with Iosif Simonov, the brotherhood's highest ranking mob member. The man who had personally ordered Professor Alan Thomas's death. She wondered briefly if he even remembered who Alan Thomas was or the destruction his death had caused the woman he'd loved and left behind.

She saw Carey's face in her mind and felt a sharp pain in the vicinity of her heart. She hadn't seen Carey in over a year and a half when she had walked out of Elena's office after she'd regretfully told Carey no arrest would ever be made in regards to her husband's murder. That the man who had ordered the hit was untouchable and she had to make do with the lackey who'd performed the deed who was now dead, a victim himself who'd been found floating in the Moska river.

She could still see Carey in her mind, a young woman of twenty-four and widowed. Her corkscrew red hair just brushed her shoulders, her blue-green eyes held unshed tears. She had tried to be brave but Elena had seen the pain behind her eyes.

Carey Madigan-Thomas was an art history graduate who had married her professor before relocating with him to Russia to catalogue the artifacts inside the Kremlin Armory. While there, Carey had discovered that over twenty percent of the artifacts were fakes and had immediately gone to the authorities. It was soon learned the Mafiya had been making copies of the treasures inside the Armory and substituting them. She had learned the hard way never to cross the Brotherhood. She had lost her husband and was made to watch helplessly as Alan was tortured and ultimately killed.

Elena had received flowers and a sympathy card from Carey, though, after news of Nikolai's violent death reached her. Most likely from Carey's contacts within the museum and art world in Moscow, and if memory served correctly Carey had been settling back home in the United States at the time.

Elena had never gotten close to a witness or victim before Carey. But there was something about Carey and her situation that had hit home for Elena. It had been Alan's death that had made Elena think about Nikolai and what she would do if something ever happened to him. She had seen the devastation on Carey's face as her world crumbled and looked into her future without knowing it.

Elena sensed movement nearby and glanced up

at Lucas. *That's right*, she thought. It's here and now and they had bigger problems. What happened with Carey and Alan Thomas was long over.

She was still mad with him and knew she was being unreasonable but that bust had been the only chance to take down the Mafiya and maybe get justice for Alan, Carey, and countless others whose lives had been touched by the Brotherhood. Now that was gone.

"Are you all right?" he asked.

Elena nodded. "Yes. No. He's a horrible, sadistic man. I've seen what he does to people. Or should I say has done to them. One case in particular is always in my mind. A friend's husband, the museum friend I told you about. Her husband was tortured and murdered in front of her eyes." Elena shook her head savagely, clearing her thoughts and the horrific crime scene that sprung to mind. "They'll never get justice and Simonov will never pay for his crimes."

Lucas rubbed the back of his neck with his hand. "I really am sorry. I didn't think of the repercussions."

She shrugged. "No, you were right. We have more pressing concerns at the moment then Simonov and the Mafiya. Like who killed Nikolai and Pochenchov and why. We're still no closer to learning who is involved and in what exactly. How are we supposed to fight something we can't see?"

She pinched the bridge of her nose in frustration. She was tired and hungry and cold. She was scared and the cold only served to make her more miserable. Lucas was always in her thoughts followed by guilt of thinking of another man when she'd only just recently lost the man she had pledged her life to. What would Nikolai think of her? She only hoped he wasn't looking down on her at the moment, her mind and body filled with desire over a man she barely knew who was constantly surprising her and pushing her to new limits. He frustrated her, annoyed her, and comforted her. She shivered at the memory of Lucas's arms wrapped around her and her body ached to relive that experience.

***

Lucas swung his arm around Elena's shoulders and pulled her close and probably surprised the both of them when he placed a kiss on her forehead. It was fast becoming a regular gesture to soothe her, he realized, and he enjoyed it way too much.

He had never been an overly demonstrative man—except when it came to sex—and certainly didn't have a romantic bone in his body, but with Elena he found he wanted to be. He wanted to touch her for the sheer sake of being close, her skin against his own, breathing her scent into his lungs.

She exhaled loudly and softened against him. He wondered briefly what else he could make her body do before pushing away all thoughts of Elena naked. With the freezing temperature, he was likely to snap off any stiff, protruding parts of his body. Besides, the ring on her finger was enough of a reminder to him that she was taken. It didn't matter that the man was dead, Elena was still very much married in her mind. He respected that, once more thinking what it would be like to have the love of a woman like Elena.

He supposed that was why he'd never fully committed to any of his previous relationships. His subconscious had been waiting for a woman like Elena. A woman he could trust who was loyal. Too bad she was taken. But he was happy to accept friendship as second best. He found he liked being with her without sex being foremost in his mind. She was smart, witty, sometimes sassy, and had a temper to rival Fitzgibbon's. He enjoyed uncovering different facets to her being and getting to know her. Nikolai had been one lucky guy.

"I know. I'm frustrated too," he told her as he scanned the empty street. They needed to get someplace warm while they regrouped and thought of their next move. He spotted an establishment still open and started towards it, Elena falling into step with him. "Come on in here and we'll rest."

He hauled her into a darkened nightclub. The interior looked like the setting for some vampire movie. He soon understood why when he saw the Goth-looking strippers, several of whom were taking their customers behind dark curtains to perform private shows for them. He involuntarily shuddered and thought he should get Elena out of there as quickly as possible. When he turned to suggest they leave, the words died on his lips. Even the garish glow that spilled out from the small porcelain sconces on the wall highlighted the dark circles under her beautiful grey eyes. He decided against seeking out another establishment, worried

Elena might not make it until he found them a safe place—wherever that was—to lay low. His gut burned knowing he was the cause of it. She didn't appear to notice her surroundings as she flopped down in a booth in the back where there was nobody around, all the partygoers up front or in a private room.

He watched as she took in the room around her and was surprised at the lack of emotion on her face. He had been expecting disgust or anger and found nothing but a blank slate. She was either too far gone to care or she was used to seeing this kind of thing.

He sat back and thought about their current situation. It had all started over six months ago when Nikolai Nagregor arrested one of Alvin Pochenchov's buddies. Lucas assumed the man had traded information with Nagregor for a leaner sentence. Now Nikolai knew something and was bound by his ethics to investigate. What he found had ultimately led to his death and he was murdered to keep that intel safe. Intel that he believed involved some sort of incendiary device what with Ducane's involvement.

"What I don't understand is why they killed Nikolai before finding what they were looking for. What the hell did Nikolai have that they wanted so badly?"

He expressed his concerns out loud. It was what he would do being in the same circumstances as their perpetrator. There was no valid or sensible reason to kill the one man with the answers, particularly one who had something important to lose, like Elena.

She gave it some thought. "I honestly don't know. I never saw Nikolai with anything. At least nothing that stood out as important."

"I doubt it would be something that would jump out at you. If the information is as important as I think, it'll be hidden in something innocuous." He pinned Elena's eyes with his, weariness reflected in the cool depths. "Where would Nikolai hide something he was afraid someone was after?"

He thought about his training and wondered where he might hide something he didn't want found by the wrong people. He also added in the factor that Nikolai knew it was someone in the intelligence field, so he would have been overly cautious about where he hid his intel. The usual locations were out of the picture. The man would have been exceedingly paranoid.

Elena's brow furrowed. "Trained people couldn't find it, so what makes you think I'd know?"

"You were his wife," he stated matter-of-factly.

Chapter 20

A waitress walked over to them and they put their conversation on hold. Elena immediately asked for a strong drink. She needed it after the night she had. To think when she had arrived at work yesterday morning she had sighed at the mountain of paperwork on her desk and thought it was going to be a normal day. She had been happy and excited when Vladimir had finally taken her off probation. Never once did she think the day would end up like this, sitting in a strip club with a man she hardly knew, talking about a conspiracy that involved Nikolai's murder and the possibility of rogue agents in her agency.

Better make that a double, she thought and told the waitress.

The waitress smiled at them before returning to the bar. If she thought it odd that a man *and* a woman had walked into the club, she didn't let it show. Elena shivered at the thought that men might find it a turn-on to watch this kind of thing with their partners. She and Nikolai certainly never needed help in that department.

She looked about the room again, relieved to see she was the only female other than the dancers and waitresses. She also noted there wasn't a TV, so with any luck they would not be recognized. Not that they were in danger of being so, she thought as she watched the red-lipped, raven haired and black stiletto wearing burlesque dancers on stage performing their seductive moves designed to entice and excite. No one was looking in their direction and if questioned later wouldn't be able to confirm or deny that she and Lucas had been there, let alone pick them out of a line-up.

Elena turned back to face Lucas. He was watching her closely, too closely. A blush rose from her neck and she wondered if he had noticed her watching the dancers and what he thought. She sat back in her seat and away from the glare of the light above the booth in an effort to hide her heated face. She had already embarrassed herself enough with her crying fit earlier. She didn't need Lucas to see her blushing as well.

"We don't have to stay here, if you'd like to go someplace else?" he offered.

Elena shook her head. "No, really, it's fine. I don't mind. I just don't understand the allure."

Lucas shrugged. "You and me both."

She raised an eyebrow. "Really? You don't find this," she searched for the right word, "appealing?"

Lucas gave the room a sweeping glance before turning back to her. "No, I don't. I prefer to use my imagination."

He held her gaze, and her body warmed and it

wasn't from the atmosphere in the sordid establishment. She got the feeling he was looking through her clothes to the skin below and her nipples pebbled. She felt an answering throb between her thighs and cursed the unwanted attraction she felt towards him. She forced herself to look away and luckily the waitress was on her way back with their drinks. She needed to cool down.

The waitress returned and Elena paid her, the cash reserves they desperately needed quickly dwindling. It would soon become another problem. The waitress moved away to take more orders.

"Getting back to what we were talking about," she picked up her glass and took a sip, feeling the burn as the vodka slid down her throat, "what does my being Nikolai's wife have to do with anything?"

"He would have trusted you," Lucas stated simply.

She frowned. Nikolai played things close to the chest. If he didn't want you to know something, torture couldn't drag it from his mouth.

"I don't know about that," she said. "For all you know, Nikolai could have *suspected* me."

***

Lucas shook his head, immediately disregarding what she said. There was no way anyone could suspect Elena of any wrongdoing. She wore her heart on her sleeve and every emotion was plain to see on her face. Like before when she had been blushing. He had almost leaned across the table to give her something to blush about. He mentally shook his head to get back on track. She was seriously messing with his ability to stay focused— well, on anything but her.

"No, he would've trusted you," he declared passionately.

She glanced at him in surprise. "Why are you so sure about that?"

He looked into her cool grey eyes and replied, "Because I trust you, and I doubt good old Nikolai would've thought differently. You're an honest woman, Elena, one who wouldn't give up her morals for the chance at money or power."

Lucas saw her eyes mist over and cursed himself. He watched as she took another sip of her drink, trying once more to conceal her feelings from him. Her diamond wedding ring stuck out proudly from her finger. She must have loved Nikolai very much. To wear his ring months after his death, announcing to the world that she still belonged to him. He wondered again what it would be like to have someone so devoted to the memory of him.

He only had Jim and Maggie to mourn him and would exist only as an anonymous star on the wall at Langley. He was so distracted thinking of his pitiful existence that he'd almost missed it and went still as Elena brought her hand up, through the bright white light above their booth. His eyes narrowed and locked on her finger, following her hand as it went back down to the table as she replaced her glass. *No*, he thought. It couldn't be that simple, but he knew without a doubt it was. They may be worlds apart, but he and Nikolai were both schooled in the art of intelligence. He looked up from Elena's hand. She wore a look of concern and figured she must have been talking to him.

"Sorry, what did you say?"

Elena frowned. "I said, is everything all right?"

He nodded, looking at her ring again. "Your wedding ring. May I see it?"

Her eyebrow arched. She probably wondered why he wanted to see it but she didn't ask. She slid the ring off her finger and handed it over to him. Like a jeweler, he studied the rock from each angle, scrutinizing it. Up close he could see the stone was not actually a diamond, which he had guessed previously. Satisfied, he put it on the table, raised his glass, drained it then brought it down hard on the gold band where it met with the stone. The rock fell loose from its mooring.

Elena jumped up. "What did you do that for?"

She snatched up her ring and the faux diamond. He thought he heard her swear under her breath. She looked downright murderous and thought it best to explain fast.

"Elena, it's not your ring."

Her eyes widened. Shocked, she stared down at the two pieces in her hand. Lucas took the stone from her palm and held it to the light. Her eyes changed and she sat down heavily in her seat.

She exhaled heavily. "Oh my God, is that a…" Her voice faded.

Lucas completed the sentence for her. "Data crystal? I believe so. I can just make out some markings inside. Nikolai must have switched your ring."

She shook her head. "How? When?"

"Sometime before he died. He must have known the information he had was dangerous. He didn't tell you because he didn't want them to target you."

She sat there fuming, her face flushed with anger. "It's so frustrating. Who is 'them'? I'm sick of calling them by ominous names. We should know who they are and what their agenda is. If only my freaking agency would pull their heads out of their asses long enough to see what's going on."

Lucas couldn't stop his eyebrows from rising high towards his hair line. When Elena erupted it was tantamount to Mount St. Helen's. He watched as she let out a deep breath, her chest rising and falling heavily from the exertion of her outburst. Her red face returned to its normal shade as the flames were put out. It was quite fascinating to him how she could contain such fire burning inside of her and wondered if it spilled over to other areas of her life as well.

She sat in silence, looking down at the gold wedding band and crystal on her palm.

"How...how did you know?" she asked.

"The wedding photo in your apartment," he explained. "The sun shined directly on the diamond, casting a rainbow of colors. Just then, when the light was on your ring...nothing."

She nodded. "I must have been wearing this ring for over six months and I never noticed."

He lifted the crystal to the light. He had heard of data crystals but they weren't widely available, at least not yet. Give it a couple of years and they'd be the next hot thing. Lucas had an idea of how they worked, had watched the technology gurus at

Langley showcase their design. He vaguely remembered something about each piece of data being ingrained onto multiple 3-D holographic sheets. He should have paid better attention.

"Do you think you can read the data?"

Elena frowned. "If it is not too damaged, yes."

He squinted at the crystal. "Well, we won't be able to read this at any internet café."

Elena nodded, looking over at the crystal like it was some mathematical problem. "No, we're going to need some high tech stuff. I know someone who can help."

"He doesn't work for SVR, does he?" he asked.

"No."

He gave it some thought. He looked her in the eye, reading her face like a book. "Do you trust him?"

Elena nodded. "Explicitly."

He stood up. "Okay then, that's good enough for me. Let's go."

Chapter 21

James Fitzgibbon was not in a good mood. He should be home right now with his wife, Maggie, eating her succulent roast turkey dinner but instead he was in his plain office, which overlooked a damn parking lot of all fucking things, trying to calm down the Russian Director. He wasn't appreciated nearly enough as he should be. When this was all over, he was taking Maggie on a nice long vacation to the Bahamas or some such place she was always gushing about.

What the hell have you gotten yourself into now, Gates?

He leaned back in his chair. Lucas had killed a Russian agent. Not only that, he had escaped and taken another along with him, through the streets of Moscow resisting arrest and tearing up the place. *A typical day for Gates.* On the last count, he had stolen one car and evaded the authorities and endangered innocent citizens.

He ran his fingers through his hair. Lucas was known to be rather spontaneous in his pursuits but something didn't sit right with this investigation. It hadn't from its inception. But why had he taken his liaison officer with him? Was she in on the plot or whatever the hell was going on? Or was she helping him? It could only be one or the other, knowing Lucas. He prayed it was the latter. The man could use all the help he could get. He had to find some way to get in contact with his man and find out his side of the story before they had an international incident on their hands. Or at least more than they already had. *Damn Gates*. He should've gone with Austin. At least he didn't make it his life's work to cause grief and give him migraines.

He picked up his phone and dialed the number by heart. He hated canceling on Maggie. She was always so patient with his job and took a lot in stride. Even after she'd slaved so long to create the delicious meal that would be cold by the time he got to it. She wasn't going to like it when he told her he wouldn't be home for dinner, but he had work to do and that came above all else. Besides, Maggie liked Lucas, so she would understand.

He hoped.

Chapter 22

Lucas followed Elena down the darkened street to an apartment complex in the area of Belorusskaya-Radialnaya where her computer friend lived. It had taken them over an hour to navigate the city despite the late hour, even after he'd used his gadget to unlock another car, this one a dark blue Ford Focus which they'd left several blocks south in case of discovery.

Elena pulled her coat more securely around her body as she stopped in front of the small speaker box mounted on the wall beside the front steel door. She pressed the button he assumed corresponded with the correct apartment above. They only had to wait a minute before a wide-awake voice came wafting out. *"Da?"* was the response.

"Dmitry, it is Elena," she spoke in English, probably for his benefit. "I have a computer problem for you."

If the recipient, Dmitry, thought it strange she was speaking in English, he didn't voice his opinion. A buzzer sounded angrily as if protesting the time of night. Elena opened the heavy door to the complex and started towards the elevator. Lucas noticed briefly the niceness of the apartment building that probably cost a mint. The computer specialist obviously made some dough. Clean teal carpet lined the floor and the painted walls were done in tasteful mocha and lined with framed black and white panoramic views of Moscow.

The elevator door opened on level three and Lucas trailed behind Elena down a long hallway and around a corner. A man still dressed in jeans and a polo shirt as if the time was two in the afternoon as opposed to two in the morning, stood in the doorway of an open apartment. His face widened with a smile when he caught sight of Elena.

"Elena," he embraced her before allowing her and Lucas to enter. The apartment was styled the same as the hallway, beautifully rendered and expertly designed. It was a long way from IKEA. Lucas took in the polished mahogany furniture. The only difference he could see between the fancy corridor and the trendy apartment was that the residence was obviously occupied by a man. There were empty beer cans and pizza boxes on the coffee table, an odd sock or two lying about and roughly twenty thousand dollars' worth of computer equipment taking up most of the space in the large open room directly ahead of him.

Dmitry turned to Elena, his English flawless. "I've heard all about you on the police band, wanted by SVR and all that." He shook his head, mock scolding her. Lucas could see Dmitry found the whole thing quite hilarious.

Elena's hands went to her hips. "Dmitry, you know you're not supposed to have a police band. What if you get caught?"

Dmitry rolled his eyes which only appeared to make Elena madder. Her left foot began to tap in a repetitious beat that Lucas recognized from his childhood as one his mother would often do when he'd done something he wasn't supposed to. His poor mother had often tapped her foot at him. He had always been surprised the thing hadn't fallen off. At this point he was expected to promise her that he'd never to do it again, which they both knew he would most likely do the moment her back was turned.

"Oh, come on, Elena," Dmitry argued. "We both know I can always hack into your agency's mainframe to get information. If I was caught, which offense do you think would get me less time? Besides, it's more fun than Satellite." He turned to Lucas. "Am I right?"

"Don't encourage him," Elena said before making the introductions. "Lucas Gates, Dmitry Ivanov—my little brother."

Dmitry's eyes widened as he took in Lucas as if he had only just realized they weren't alone in the room. He studied Lucas's face before saying, "Nice hat."

"Hey," Elena said, slapping Dmitry on the shoulder. "I bought that for him."

Lucas grinned. "There's no accounting for the woman's taste."

Dmitry shook his head. "I don't know about that. Have you seen her apartment?" He suddenly became serious, his face changing in an instant. "You're the American right, the one the SVR is after?"

Lucas nodded and held out his hand. "Hope you don't hold it against me for getting your sister involved in this mess," he said, looking in the man's eyes. Elena's cool grey ones looked back at him. It was definitely the same man from the wedding photo.

Dmitry grinned, looking younger when he did so. "Knowing Elena, she probably brought it on herself."

"I most certainly did not, Dmitry. Why would you say that?" Elena's automatic defense of herself came from the kitchen where she had disappeared to after introducing the two men.

Dmitry and Lucas smiled at each other, their smiles quickly disappearing when Elena returned carrying three mugs of coffee on a tray along with some biscuits she must have found in Dmitry's pantry. She handed them each a mug and then offered some biscuits. Dmitry declined and he and Elena gobbled them all up. He hadn't realized just how hungry he was.

"So what have you got for me?" Dmitry's face turned serious again. It was amazing how versatile he was. He was probably only a couple years younger than Elena. Lucas put him at around twenty-six. Where Elena was fair haired, Dmitry's was dark, almost black. He was tall, only an inch shorter than himself, and they both towered over Elena. He could just imagine some of the horrible things Dmitry would've done to Elena growing up as only a little brother could. Although Lucas didn't have any siblings, he knew what boys got up to and he and his best mate had always teased the boy's sister. They even had competitions on seeing who could make her cry first. He had been terrible to the girl.

Lucas brought out the small data crystal and Dmitry frowned as Lucas placed it in his palm.

"Do you think you can read it?" he asked.

"I'll give it a go," Dmitry said. "It may take some time, so if you want to get some rest, I'll wake you if I find anything."

Elena smiled at her brother. "Thanks. I might do that after I take a shower. I feel horrible."

The idea of Elena in the shower sent blood coursing hotly through Lucas's veins. Why did she have to bring that up? It was sure to put ideas in his head. Not that they weren't there already. He could see so clearly Elena standing in the shower, wet all over, soap suds sliding down her body. Lucas wanted to climb in with her and run his hands all over her flawless skin, lick away the beads of water resting on her shoulders. He could feel himself growing hard and knew at once he had to move away from the fantasy. He shook his head, clearing the erotic images playing through his mind.

Elena collected the empty mugs and returned them to the kitchen before wandering down the hall to the bathroom. Lucas settled himself on the couch nearby the studious Dmitry and stretched his legs out. He was just drifting off when he heard Dmitry's voice.

"You're going to get my sister out of this, aren't

you?"

He opened his eyes and turned his head to face Dmitry, looking into the eyes just like Elena's and said very clearly, "Yes I am."

Dmitry nodded. "I thought so. You seem the type to finish what you started, but I had to make sure. Elena's the only family I have left since Nikolai died. I don't want to lose her too, for any reason," he added.

Lucas could see the brotherly concern for Elena on Dmitry's face. He could see they were close, the two of them alone in the world with only each other to rely on. Lucas liked Dmitry instantly from that moment. The guy would do just about anything for his sister.

"Did she love him a lot?"

He immediately regretted the impromptu question when Dmitry raised an eyebrow. He knew what the man must be thinking and hated the fact that he'd left himself as open as a book.

"Yeah, she did," Dmitry answered, not asking the question that was clear as day on his face. "The thing is, with Elena, she loves whole-heartedly. It's amazing to be on the receiving end of such unconditional love."

Lucas didn't disagree. Elena was one hell of a woman. *One in a million*, he thought, recalling the night's previous events. Not many women would have risked everything to help him. Few would have put up with the scenic drive around Moscow, and to top everything off, a visit to the unfriendly neighborhood mob. He was still annoyed with himself about that.

He heard the shower cut off down the hall. After a few minutes, the door to the bathroom opened and they heard Elena ask, "Dmitry, do you still have some of Olga's clothes?"

Dmitry looked towards the bathroom. "Yeah, in a box in the spare room," he replied, turning back around and catching Lucas's eye. A blush rose from his face and Lucas pretended not to notice. "An ex-girlfriend," he explained. "Haven't had a chance to get rid of her clothes."

Lucas nodded, having had to remove the clothing of ex-girlfriends from his home on more than one occasion.

"I've never understood how they can spread their shit so far, then forget to take it with them when they leave," he commiserated with a fellow male.

Dmitry nodded. "Elena's not like that, though," he added.

Lucas wasn't sure why Dmitry felt the need to divulge Elena's housekeeping habits, so he kept quiet and soon was fast asleep on the couch.

Chapter 23

Dmitry turned his full attention to the photo-refractive crystal. He was fascinated and loved a good challenge. He hadn't found any computer system yet he couldn't crack, although he liked to think of himself as a grey hat, using his powers for fun and thrill not thieving or terrorism. He made quite a bit of money in the private sector designing software for businesses around the country. He also designed web security programs along with spyware and Trojans. He loved experimenting with certain systems, seeing what worked and what didn't.

He turned as his sister approached. Elena glanced over at Lucas asleep on the couch. His mouth was slightly open, yet he was pleased to note devoid of drool. His head was on an angle which didn't look comfortable but Lucas didn't seem to mind. He was probably so exhausted he could have slept standing up.

"You know you're not cheating on Nikolai, right?" he asked softly, sensing the attraction between the two. He had liked Nikolai, thought of him as a brother, but he wanted nothing more than to see his older sister happy and if the American currently conked out on his couch did it for her, then he was glad.

Elena turned her shocked grey eyes on him. "What?"

Dmitry shrugged. "I see the way you're looking at him. Don't think I haven't noticed. The air around you two is charged."

She made a dismissing motion with her hands. "No, it's not." She looked over at Lucas nervously. His eyes remained closed, his breathing regular. Dmitry doubted if the Russian National Orchestra playing *Swan Lake* would wake him.

"Relax, Elena, he's dead to the world...and yes." He caught her eyes. "Yes, it is. You did what you said you'd do. Until death do you part. I know you think that that's all you get, but it's not."

He'd watched his sister fall apart after Nikolai's death and had wished to ease her pain somehow, knowing full well he couldn't. Slowly she had begun to heal but still she had not gone back into the world of dating. He had tried on several occasions to get her to come out with him but she had declined each time. He was surprised when he had felt the vibes bouncing back and forth between her and Lucas. He hadn't seen Elena show any man interest in a long time.

"I love Nikolai, Dmitry. Now drop it."

"There's all kinds of love. Just because you love Nikolai does not mean you can't fall for Lucas. I know you like him and it's the same for him."

Elena frowned. "He said that?" She again looked

over at Lucas as if expecting him to answer her question.

He followed her gaze. Lucas wasn't exactly the type of man he saw for Elena—another Nikolai—but that appeared to be the kind she was attracted to and Lucas seemed like a good guy. The kind you could trust. A man whose word and promise meant everything. He believed Lucas when he said he would get Elena out of the mess she was in.

"He didn't have to. It's written all over his face, Elena. Remember, I'm a guy too. I know what a man looks like when he's interested in a female."

It may have been a while since he had looked at any woman like that, but he knew the signs and they were all there. Lucas most certainly had the hots for Elena. He was surprised the room didn't burst into flames when Lucas looked at her. He also seemed the type to be possessive of his woman and protect her no matter what.

"To sleep with me, maybe," Elena said, denying any deep feelings she and Lucas may have for each other.

He grinned. "More than likely," he conceded. He wasn't stupid enough to assume Lucas's intentions were entirely honorable. "But I think it's more than that and what's more, I see what he's doing to you. You're happy even with the entire government on your ass and the situation you're in. I haven't seen you like this since before Nikolai died. You're practically glowing. It would be hard not to notice."

And she was. That was the strangest part. He practically needed sunglasses just to look at her. Any man who could bring her back into the world of the living was okay in his books.

"Shouldn't you be working on that crystal thingy?" she said, deflecting from the issue, looking closely at the crystal.

"I'm taking a page out of your book, Elena, and I'm *multi-tasking*," he said, the word foreign to him, tasting it.

Elena flopped down on the stool beside him and watched as he begun the extensive process of retrieving the data from the crystal, sending monochromatic light beams into certain angles of the crystal and retrieving the data. It would take some time to sort out the layers of 3-D holographic images he collected. He heard Elena let out a reluctant sigh.

"I admit I like him but it can't go anywhere."

He didn't look up at her, figuring she would do better to bare her soul if it was more like confession, giving up her dirty secrets anonymously. All alone in the darkness without spectators waiting to scrutinize every word spoken and action made.

"Because of Nikolai?"

She shrugged. "Partly...mostly. Besides the last twenty-four hours have been a blur of nothing but adrenaline and anxiety. No, it's impossible and you know it." He heard her voice begin to rise as she began to work herself up, her breath leaving her mouth in agitated puffs. "Even if I did want to, and I'm not saying I do. But he's going to go back to America in a few days and that'll be it."

Would it, Elena?

"You could always follow him," he suggested.

She shook her head. "Even if I thought we'd have a chance, I could never leave you. You're the only family I have left."

He knew she would say that. Frankly, he thought it was just an excuse on her part. Fear of the unknown. His sister had never been much of an adventurer. In this day and age of email and airplanes, keeping in touch was easy. She was just scared and refused to admit it to herself.

"You could if you were willing to take the leap."

Elena crossed her arms beneath her breasts in a defensive gesture and glared at him.

"Don't start, Dmitry."

He knew he wouldn't be able to get through to her. She had built up a nice wall around her heart and would most likely die before she would listen to reason. Her Russian stubbornness really came out when she was cornered. He decided to let the subject drop right after he got the last word in.

He shrugged. "Fine. Be an ostrich. The only one you're hurting is yourself. I just don't want you to look back one day and say 'what if.' I loved Nikolai, Elena, but your life shouldn't end just because his did."

Chapter 24

Lucas could smell lavender. He slowly opened his eyes and blinked the cobwebs away. For a moment, he forgot where he was. He could feel the kink in his neck and attempted to dislodge it. He wondered how long he had been asleep. His eyes felt gritty and he raised his hand to his face and rubbed at his eyes to remove the sleep before sliding his hand over his jaw. He felt the stubble poking his callused palm. His gaze fell on Dmitry, who amazingly looked as if he had slept for eight hours. Only the creases in his clothes and the five o'clock shadow darkening the bottom of his face was any indication he hadn't rested.

Elena stood beside her brother. They were both at eye level now that Dmitry was sitting. Her light hair hung loosely about her shoulders. She was dressed in dark blue jeans and a white fitted top, her delicate feet bare, and he could see the pale baby pink nail polish on her toenails. She was where the lavender smell was coming from, another leftover item from an ex-girlfriend Dmitry neglected to throw away. That, or he just liked the scent, which was currently growing on Lucas as was the person who wore it.

"What time is it?" he croaked. His mouth was dry from sleep. He ran his tongue over his furry teeth. He really needed to spend some time on hygiene.

Dmitry and Elena both turned toward him.

"Nine-thirty," Dmitry replied after consulting the time and date in the taskbar of his computer.

He'd had a good six hours of sleep. He felt somewhat refreshed, and the rest would be solved by a hot mug of strong coffee.

"We thought it best to let you sleep," Elena said.

Dmitry rolled his eyes and discreetly pointed at Elena, indicating that it was in fact *her* who thought it best. The thought of Elena caring about him sent his stomach into flips. It had been some time since anyone other than Jim or Maggie had cared for his well-being.

"Big momma bear, this one," Dmitry said, nodding towards Elena. "She wouldn't let me disturb you."

He was wide awake now and got to his feet in one swift motion. "You found something?"

Dmitry nodded, looking pleased. "I did indeed."

He walked over to them, trying to avoid smelling the alluring lavender. He frowned at what he saw on the computer screen. There were several windows open on the desktop and what he was seeing was a bunch of squiggly lines and Russian characters. He knew he wasn't the brightest bulb in the box but what the hell was he looking at?

"Is that everything?"

Elena nodded. "Dmitry uploaded all the data about an hour ago."

Lucas once again took in the computer screen. Dmitry clicked the mouse a few times, changing the image on the screen into a clockwise position and altering the contrast of the pixels. A blueprint of an old building set out in an elongated rectangle came into focus.

"Do either of you recognize that building?" he asked them.

Elena and Dmitry both looked at each other and nodded.

"Well?" he demanded, knowing he was missing something significant.

"The Winter Palace in St. Petersburg," Dmitry finally said.

Lucas frowned. Why put the detailed plan of the palace on a crystal for safe keeping. Why was it so important? He assumed you couldn't just get it anywhere, but wasn't it a tourist spot, famous for being the last residence of the royal family or something? He really should've spent more time listening in history class instead of gazing at the girl who'd sat in the row in front of him. He ran his stiff fingers through his hair.

"I don't get it. What would be the point of blowing up the Palace?" he wondered aloud.

"Millions of people visit the palace and connecting State Hermitage Museum every year. It could just be the volume of people. You've said earlier that Ducane has killed before," Elena pondered.

"I just don't feel like we're on the right track," he said.

Dmitry asked the question they were all thinking. "Then why would Nikolai go to so much trouble as to put it on the crystal?"

They all stood there in silence until Lucas broke it. He squinted his eyes at the scribble on screen. "What's that?" he asked, pointing to the tiny lettering.

Dmitry used his mouse to make it bigger.

"It's a date, the seventh of November."

Elena frowned. "That's today. Whatever Nikolai knew was going to happen is occurring now."

"What else do you have?" he asked Dmitry.

Dmitry clicked his mouse button. He quickly sorted through the rest of the data he had collected from the crystal. "Besides the map? An itinerary. Does that help? I can't make out any more."

He frowned. "An itinerary?"

Dmitry nodded.

"Zimtovich," Elena said softly. He could hear the disappointment in her voice. "That bastard. He was selling information."

Lucas didn't feel the need to comment. He had already figured that out long ago. What he couldn't wrap his head around was what it all meant. What did one get when they added a schematic to a museum, an itinerary, a few dead Russians, a known terrorist or two, and a weapons trader? Frustrated, he said, "For what, though?"

Elena turned to her brother. "Could you find out where this year's UN summit is being held and when?"

Dmitry nodded. "Sure just give me a minute." He pulled up *Google.ru*, Russia's Search Engine, and started typing in the search field.

"What are you thinking?" he asked, his gaze never leaving her face. He could tell she was on to something. Her body practically vibrated with excited energy.

"I should've picked up on it before but my mind was locked on Moscow."

"What are you talking about?" Lucas asked.

Elena huffed out a deep breath. "Remember when you asked me why red flags didn't come up when Ducane entered the country and I replied that it was impossible to monitor everyone at the moment?"

"Yeah, something about Grand Central Station and the UN Summit," he replied, still unsure as to what was going through her mind.

She rolled her eyes at what he had taken away from their conversation. That seemed like so long ago rather than just the day before last. So much had happened since that time in her office.

"Yes, delegates from all over have been flying into Moscow and St. Petersburg for days now. You were lucky to get a seat when you did."

Lucas gave it some thought. Luck wasn't quite what he would call it but then it had led him to Elena so it wasn't all that bad. Dmitry swore. He was beginning to remember the word. It seemed a favorite of Elena's and apparently Dmitry's.

"What?" he asked.

Dmitry turned to him. "The UN Summit is being held on November seventh at four in the afternoon at the Winter Palace in St. Petersburg," he announced. "It's quite the fanfare. The annual peace conference coincides with the anniversary of the revolution."

Lucas couldn't believe it. Everything fell together thanks to Nikolai Nagregor getting them the information from beyond the grave.

Way to go out with a bang!

He could visualize Nikolai standing there, confronting his assassin, gun in hand saying, "Yippee ki-yay…"

"We have to get there. What's the fastest way to St. Petersburg?" Lucas asked the natives. The pieces of the puzzle were not coming together quickly enough for his liking.

This was why Michael Ducane was here and it made Lucas sick to his stomach. How many people would lose their lives if he failed today? Hundreds? Thousands? People who were trying to make the world a better place. That was the kicker and that was why Ducane needed the government mole. With such a high profile event, security would be crawling all over the palace. It would be hard to smuggle in a bomb without the proper help.

Elena answered, "Fly, but I wouldn't recommend it. SVR will be all over us."

"That's not all, Lucas," Dmitry interrupted them, his voice foreboding.

Lucas let out a long suffering sigh. Could things get any worse?

"What is it?"

"Check out who will be at the summit."

He and Elena moved closer to the computer

screen before he realized he couldn't read the Russian letters, so instead he watched Elena's face frown as she read. Dmitry put his finger on the screen, pointing to where she needed to read. Lucas watched the blood drain from her face. She looked over at him and he prepared himself to catch her should she faint. He figured a light wind would knock her off her feet.

"Well, who is it?"

"Sergei Smirnov," she whispered.

Lucas raised an eyebrow. Whoever this Sergei Smirnov was, he was in big fucking trouble.

"Our president," Dmitry elaborated. "And he won't be alone. Your President will also be there. Air Force One touched down in St. Petersburg earlier this morning."

Fuck. Lucas remembered Jim telling him about the president visiting but he hadn't realized it would be so soon. This was not good. He had to talk to Fitzgibbon, let him know what was the fuck was happening. Maybe he could do something from his end. Jim was, after all, rather resourceful and hoarded favors like some people collected baseball cards. He would have a contact somewhere that could surely warn the Secret Service.

"We have to get to St. Petersburg."

Elena nodded. She had obviously been thinking the exact same thing. "We'll have to leave right away. It takes approximately four hours by train from Moscow."

Lucas did the math in his head. They would barely have enough time.

Dmitry turned back to his computer and deftly

brought up the railway's website. He typed quickly on the keyboard, found the tickets he was after and clicked on 'buy now' with his mouse.

"You can't use a credit card, Dmitry. Who knows how far SVR have gone with their manhunt," Elena warned. "They might have flagged your information as well as mine."

"No worries, Elena," Dmitry said as he continued to fill in the pertinent information, using aliases for him and Elena. "I'll just use the dummy account I set up, untraceable even by the Russian Government."

There was a hint of pride in his voice, no arrogance, just fact. Dmitry knew he was good and obviously had the skills to back up the claim.

"Dmitry, why do you have a dummy account?" Elena asked. Her hands once again went to her hips and her eyes narrowed. Oh boy. She certainly looked pissed. Lucas would hate to be in Dmitry's shoes right now. He had seen many women pissed. Most of the time at him, but the way Elena was looking right now was way past his experience. She practically had steam coming out her ears. This could turn into a long discussion. He placed a gentle hand on her arm.

"Another time?" he said, and relief appeared on Dmitry's face when she nodded. "Go get your things ready."

Elena went to retrieve her purse from the kitchen. Lucas gave Dmitry a level look. The entire family was growing on him. God, he had no hope.

"You do realize you'll be revisiting that subject when this is all over, don't you?" he asked.

Dmitry nodded solemnly. "You'd think she'd be happy since it's come in handy in this instance."

"Women, Dmitry," Lucas said, as if that was the explanation. "You can never really tell with them."

"Don't I know it. If it's not a girlfriend, it's Elena. I get no peace. You have any sisters?"

"No, I'm an only child."

"Lucky you. Some of the time, she can really be a blessing but she can also be a—"

They broke off as Elena came back into the room. She sent Dmitry a glare and he promptly turned back to his computer, pressing the print button and announced he was done.

Elena gave her brother a smile. "You know you're wasted in the public sector, right? SVR could really use you."

"Call me crazy, Elena, but I don't particularly want to work for the agency that wants to hang you out to dry."

Elena conceded.

"One more thing, Dmitry," Lucas said. "You mind giving us a lift?"

Chapter 25

When they arrived at Moscow Leningradsky Station, Lucas and Elena hesitated in Dmitry's car. The two of them had been trying to come up with a plan on the ride over. They hadn't been able to reach an understanding.

"We should call Mishkin," Elena said.

Lucas shook his head. "What if he's involved?"

Exasperated, she glared at him. "Well, we can't exactly walk into the Summit with guns blazing, now can we? Isn't that *your* plan?"

Dmitry grinned like the Cheshire Cat. "That's rather a suicide mission, isn't it? Those FSB boys don't fool around."

"I'll call Jim," he said simply.

Elena got huffy. "And how can we trust your boss and not mine?"

He turned around in his seat and leaned close to her. "Because my boss doesn't get anything out of this either way."

"And mine does?" she said indignantly.

"We don't know that. Who are you defending,

Mishkin? Why in God's name are you defending the gnome who sent his henchmen after you?"

She sent him a look that chilled him more than the weather outside the car could ever do. Elena leaned forward and hugged her brother from the back seat.

"Take care of yourself, you hear?" he said.

She nodded. "Be good, and Dmitry? We are going to talk about that dummy account when I get home."

Lucas grinned. The woman certainly didn't let things slide. "Let's go, Elena."

She got out of the car, holding tightly to the bag containing their two guns and additional ammo and stepped out of the snow to the cover of the station. Lucas shook Dmitry's hand.

"If you don't like SVR, you can always try the CIA."

"Thank you, Lucas, I'll keep that in mind," Dmitry promised.

"You do that." He had one foot out the door when he turned back to Dmitry. "Oh, could I borrow your cell?"

Dmitry nodded and pulled the cell from his pocket. He held on tight when Lucas went to take it from him.

"Remember if anything happens to her, you my friend are going to have firsthand knowledge of playing Russian roulette. Only there'd be more than one bullet in the chamber, clear?"

Lucas nodded. "Clear. You're a good man, Dmitry. I hope I have the opportunity to see you again."

"Let's make it under better circumstances next time, shall we? *Do svidaniya,* Lucas."

"And you, Dmitry." Lucas stepped back from the car, pocketing the cell phone. He tapped the roof of the car and Dmitry drove away. Elena waved goodbye.

He joined her and together they walked into the station. They were both wearing beanies and scarves, taking care to keep their identities hidden. They were so close now. So close to the action and still had time to do something about it. He wanted nothing to interfere with their plans. Of course, that usually meant something would. They boarded first class and made their way to their private compartment, moving down the tight, almost claustrophobic corridor.

"*Do svidaniya* doesn't mean you're going to die, does it?" he asked Elena, badly mispronouncing the word.

Elena smiled. "No, it means goodbye, and its *do svidaniya,*" she replied, gently correcting him.

He opened the door to their compartment and Elena collapsed on the seat, her hair bouncing as she sat down. He took the seat across from her. She looked so clean and fresh and he could still smell the lavender. He knew it was going to drive him crazy for the next four or so hours. She leaned forward and regarded him. He wondered how she was seeing him. He probably resembled a homeless person, his hair and teeth unbrushed, his shirt and pants crinkled, yesterday's stubble on his face. He hadn't had the chance to clean himself up at Dmitry's. They'd left as soon as the ink was dry on the tickets. There had been no time to lose. They were currently on the only train that would get them to St. Petersburg before the Summit was to begin.

The snow was going to make it bad enough and the only luggage they had with them contained their two guns. He ran his hand across his mouth self-consciously and prayed his breath wasn't too bad.

"That's it," Elena said, snapping her fingers together. She smiled at him, excitement causing her cheeks to flush. "Zimtovich was SVR's liaison to FSB."

He sat there trying to make heads or tails of what she had just said. He knew she was speaking English, but the meaning was lost on him.

He frowned. She enlightened him. "FSB stands for Federal Security Service of the Russian Federation, the successor of the KGB." He nodded, understanding up to this point so she continued, "FSB is also the security for the president."

It all made sense now. He remembered she had mentioned that fact back in her office, but at the time it'd had no bearing.

"That was the plan all along, to wipe out both the American and Russian presidents. Along with half the UN summit," he added.

Elena scoffed. "That's rather ambitious."

Lucas had seen worse. "It's the perfect opportunity. Two birds, one stone."

Elena was right. It was awfully bloody ambitious and Ducane could pull it off too. That was the real scary part of the plan. Most assassination attempts were so far out of left field you weren't even in the same state anymore.

"Well, that certainly explains why Zimtovich now fits into a body bag. He simply knew too much."

"What kind of information was Zimtovich privy to?"

Elena thought for a moment. "Presidential itinerary, Secret Service escape plans, code words, even the president's bathroom breaks."

Lucas grinned. "So basically everything, the whole kit and caboodle?"

She nodded. The train pulled away from the station on route to St. Petersburg Moskovsky Station. He glanced out the window, the countryside a mash of blurs and white dots. He pulled out the cell phone he had borrowed from Dmitry and quickly worked out the time difference. Moscow was a good eight hours ahead of Washington. It would be around four am in D.C. He dialed a number from memory. Elena watched him with interest.

The phone rang several times before it was answered. The voice croaked down the phone line. "Fitzgibbon."

Lucas could tell he had just roused his boss from sleep. He prepared himself for the backlash. "Jim."

He didn't get any further. "Goddamn it, Gates. I send you to do one lousy job and you fuck it up. This has to be a new record for you."

He could hear Maggie in the background telling him to calm down and hear Lucas out. God, he loved Maggie, always the level-headed one and the only person he knew who had balls enough to tame the James Fitzgibbon beast. No one else dared to in fear of being shot or sent out on a suicide mission.

"Now, all that was blown way out of proportion, Jim. You know that."

Fitzgibbon sounded like he was going to have an aneurysm. "And you involved a Russian National while you were at it," he scolded.

"Jim, your ulcers," he heard Maggie say.

"Fuck my ulcers, Maggie. When you get your ass back here, Gates, I'm going to tear you a new one. Have you any idea the shit I've dealt with over the last forty-eight hours because of you?"

Elena's eyebrows were raised. Lucas had no doubt Elena could hear every word James was saying.

"Yeah, well, I didn't have a choice. We're fine by the way, thanks for asking."

For a moment he thought Fitzgibbon had hung up. "She's with you now?"

"Yep, and do we have a story for you. Bestseller," he told his boss and mentor as he winked at Elena who smiled back in response.

He could see the relief on her face. She probably thought Jim would hang him out to dry after the crap Mishkin had more than likely been feeding him. But he knew Fitzgibbon was made of a lot more sterner stuff. He wasn't one to charge an offense until he heard it from the horse's mouth.

Lucas started at the beginning with Nikolai's murder. He moved onto to the SVR agent he shot, to the knowledge Ducane was there to take out the Summit, and the president as well. Fitzgibbon stayed quiet the entire time. Only when Lucas finished did he speak.

"Holy fuck."

"Yeah, tell me about it. We need some help here, Jim," Lucas stated. Elena sat forward, hanging onto every word. "Pull out all those favors you have saved. We're going to need all of them. At this stage we're not sure how high this goes. I'd like to keep Mishkin in the dark until he can be confirmed either way."

"Okay, give me more info. When and where did you say this was going down?"

Lucas relayed the information to him.

"Your partner in crime doesn't have any suggestions, does she?" Jim asked.

Lucas repeated Jim's question to Elena who thought for a moment, a frown creasing her brow.

"He could try contacting—" She broke off when he handed her the phone. She took it, handling it like it was something that would bite. He almost laughed out loud at the sight.

"Hello?" she said tentatively into the phone. Lucas could hear Jim's voice booming through but couldn't make out the words from where he was sitting. At least he wasn't yelling anymore. "Yes, Special Agent Fitzgibbon, that was how it happened," her gaze found his and smiled, turning slightly in her seat to give him her shoulder. "No, sir, I made the decision on my own." He could hear laughter in her voice. "He did not coerce me in any way."

He snatched the phone from Elena. "What kind of question was that, Jim?" he growled into the phone. He could hear Jim and Maggie chuckling on the other end.

"Give me the phone, Lucas," Elena held out her hand, wiggled her fingers, and gave him a stern look. Like a naughty child who had taken something he wasn't supposed to. He placed the phone back in her hand. "I apologize for the rude interruption, sir," she said while glowering at Lucas. "Yes. I understand. Permission to shoot him if necessary. I will. Thank you, sir."

He was going to kill Jim. As soon as he got home he was going to track him down and kill him. Then he and Maggie wouldn't have to worry about the damn ulcers.

"Yes, sir, are you ready? The agent's name is Alexei Dimitrovich. He would probably be on site now. Tell him Elena Ivanova told you to contact him in regards to Nikolai Nagregor. Tell him everything that Lucas told you. He is with the FSB on presidential duty. He'll be able to remove the presidents out of harm's way."

She hung up and handed Lucas back the phone. "He's a very nice man."

Lucas glowered at her. He could see Elena and Jim getting on well with one another. They were alike in many ways. He thought it would be nice to officially introduce the two. But he doubted that would ever happen.

"You're not really going to shoot me, are you?"

She smiled. "Only if you get frisky." Lucas's eyebrow went up. She held up a hand, stopping him from speaking. "His words not mine."

He was thinking of getting frisky, that was half the problem. The scent of lavender and gardenias wafted through the air. He inhaled the sweet smell.

Everything Elena did somehow tantalized him. Aroused him. He liked how the light shined on her silky hair, how it fell on her shoulders. He remembered how it felt to touch during the brief moment when he had tucked the strands under her beanie. He imagined himself combusting if he ever touched anywhere else on her person.

"Jim should keep his mouth shut."

Elena sat back in her seat, closing her eyes. He could tell she wasn't sleeping. Her breathing was too fast. He could practically hear the gears moving inside her head.

"You're quiet," he commented.

She opened her eyes. "I was just thinking of Nikolai and how pissed off at him I am."

He raised an eyebrow. "How so?"

She wore an expression on her face that asked, 'isn't it obvious?' Perhaps it was to a woman, but try as he did, he couldn't see it.

"Nikolai had all this information and he never once shared any concerns with me about it. I mean, I would have with him. Rogue SVR agents, plots on the president. How did he think it was all going to go down?"

Lucas knew the answer right away, because Nikolai thought like him. They both had the same training, the same things ingrained inside of them from birth, the burden of being the male of the species.

"He was trying to protect you," he said simply.

Elena erupted. "How? He's dead and I have the entire government chasing me. He should have told me. We could have done something about it. I could have protected him."

She glared at him and if he'd been less of a man he would've wished to sink into oblivion just to escape her, but instead he sat there calmly. It was clear Elena needed to get a few things off her chest.

"Or you could be dead too, and then no one would know. He hid the most valuable intel he had with you, Elena. He trusted you. For men like me and what I think Nagregor was like, trust is everything."

Chapter 26

James Fitzgibbon replaced his handset back in its cradle. He had certainly called it. Maggie looked over at him with interest, her once sleepy blue eyes now wide awake. He had told her about Lucas's predicament the moment he'd gotten home. She had immediately gone on the defense, citing Lucas's many virtues. Jim hadn't realized what an altar boy Lucas was until Maggie had shared her view on the subject. She had also been intrigued with Lucas's choice of a fugitive partner and wanted to know all about Agent Elena Ivanova.

He too had been intrigued, and through his contacts he had discovered the woman to be a widow. Her husband murdered and only recently returned to work as a liaison officer when everything had turned to shit. She sounded very competent and seemed to understand her circumstances well. Elena Ivanova had also reassured him she was there of her own free will, which truthfully made him feel a whole lot better. Without a kidnapping charge, he could probably get

Lucas out of this mess.

What a damn mess Igor Zimtovich had left by being murdered in the States. The man didn't even have the decency to die on his own soil while selling out his country. He had known from the moment he was told of the dead Russian things were going to go south. He had only hoped they were far away from the investigation when it did. No such luck. He knew Lucas would do all he could to stop the attack. Lucas may have his faults despite Maggie's claims, but he was a good CIA special agent. The best. He knew what to do and how to do it and he along with Agent Ivanova were on their way to St. Petersburg now.

He glanced down at the notepad resting on his thigh, at the name Alexei Dimitrovich. It was certainly a story for Hollywood but he didn't doubt anything Lucas had told him. The threat was real and it was up to him to help. He picked up the handset once more. He had his work cut out for him. The Russians tended to be a high handed lot, denying their security was at risk without first checking and rechecking for even the slightest chance. He would have to argue with them until he was blue in the face. He let out a long suffering sigh and looked over at Maggie as she climbed out of bed.

"It sounds like it'll be a long day," she said as she put on her flannel dressing robe and tied it closed. "I'll put on some coffee."

He thanked her as she left the bedroom, her honey blond hair bouncing off her shoulders as she walked. She always seemed to know what he needed even before he did and he knew he often took Maggie for granted. She'd been an amazing wife over the past twenty years, understanding there were certain things he couldn't talk about.

She was the perfect partner. He'd not be where he is, not accomplished all that he had without her.

He found his tattered address book and opened it to the A's. Whatever the motive was behind this attack he had to find a way to stall it before it became an issue. Had to find a way to be connected with Agent Dimitrovich if he had any chance. He started dialing. The phone lines of D.C were about to light up as he called in every favor. He didn't care if he had to bribe or threaten every politician on the Hill to get results. He couldn't afford to fail. No one could. Too much rode on their success. Too many lives were in the balance and he would not have their deaths on his conscience which was already soaked with enough blood.

Chapter 27

Vladimir Mishkin's eyes burned to the point he wanted to pluck them out of his head. He had been up since the American had first shot one of his men. He was tired and irritable, his temper short. He had stretched thin his agents in a bid to locate the rogue special agent and Elena Ivanova but the American appeared resourceful beyond measure.

Had it been the United States' intention all along to appear to be doing all that they could meanwhile their agent assisted the terrorist and ensured he reached his target? It wouldn't be the first time they'd been charged of such and he was sure when it suited their needs, guilty as sin.

But in this instance Vladimir disagreed. He wasn't a supporter of the States, their country unruly but he'd meet Agent Gates. If there was ever a solid man it was him. Despite his penchant for disobeying rules and his cowboy attitude. He couldn't see the man as a rogue. Despite what he was being told.

Elena too, was loyal. She would not willingly

give up her life and career for nothing but a sure deal. Had he read the situation wrong? Nothing had sat right with him from the beginning. The quiet deafening. His gut churned with the implications. Because someone powerful enough to silence the rumors was involved.

His mind began to work. If someone was out to frame the American, they'd done a good job. For a time, even he had considered the man an enemy, especially considering the evidence presented to him. But if he took that out of the equation what was left?

Agent Gates might be the only hope either country had. A war would not benefit either country and strap Russia's already short supply of reserves. It would cripple and surely end them.

He tapped his finger impatiently against his desk.

Where were Gates and Elena? There was nowhere they could hide. Yet they continued to elude authorities. What would he do in the same position? He would finish the job he set out to do. A true patriot didn't let anything get in the way of preventing an attack.

He would not be so blind or accepting in the future. Vladimir snapped up the handset when it rang. His heart beat heavily in his chest as he listened. Finally a break. Elena had used her agency credentials in St. Petersburg to commandeer a vehicle.

What were they doing half-way across the country?

A database search later and he had his answer.

Chapter 28

She caught his eye and stopped. He winked at her from across the corridor. She waited for him to finish talking to a fellow agent. She didn't have to wait long before her tall, dark, handsome husband stepped towards her. She met him halfway. She looked into his eyes and felt herself drowning in the dark pools. He always had this effect on her. Had she met him on the street she would have thought him dangerous. Not that Nikolai wasn't dangerous, given the right circumstances—just not to her, never to her. He gave her a sexy smile as he came near, knowing what thoughts he would provoke in her mind by doing so.

She kept her face impassive.

"Am I going to be seeing you tonight?" she asked.

She noted the guilty look on his face and sighed.

"I'll be home," was all he said.

She nodded, preparing herself for yet another lonely night. She loved Nikolai but sometimes he was too dedicated to his job. She would like to spend time with him every so often. She hated feeling that way but she couldn't help thinking she wasn't a priority in her husband's eyes.

"I'll see you then."

He leaned over and kissed her. It was something he didn't often do at the office. He obviously knew he was up shit creek. She watched as he walked away, back to his office, and never once thought that would be the last time she would ever see him alive.

She had worked late that evening, time getting away from her, and when she exited the Metro station and headed towards her apartment it was long past nine.

She opened the door to her home and instinctively repelled. She knew something wasn't right and vaguely recognized the harsh scent emanating from the depths of the apartment. She could practically taste the metallic tang of blood in her mouth and fought to control her rebelling stomach. With the feeling of dread deep inside her, she moved slowly into the room. Her body quivered with knowledge she did not want to admit.

She caught sight of Nikolai face down on the floor, blood soaking the carpet around his head.

No. No. No. No. No.

Please, God no. She ran to him. There was nothing to be done for him, but her heart would not let her admit that to herself. She sank to her knees beside him, barely noticing Nikolai's cold blood seeping into her pants. Tears fell from her eyes as she took in the sight of her husband.

Elena jerked awake, her breathing harsh. Her heart pounded in her chest. She could still feel the effects of her dream, her hands quivering in shock as if she had only just found Nikolai's body. The dream was always the same, so real it felt like she was reliving the event night after night.

"You okay?"

She found Lucas watching her closely, concern on his handsome face. She nodded and leaned back against the seat in the cabin of the train.

"Yes. Just a bad dream." She swallowed. "The night I found Nikolai. It's been a while since I last had one. I guess with everything going on and with Nikolai being involved it's only natural for me to start dreaming about him again."

She stared out the window, not seeing anything. The circumstances of them being on the train returned to her, washing away the aftermath of her dream. It all seemed so out there. More like the plot of some movie than real life, her life, hers and Lucas's. She had never once thought she would end up here. She had never expected her husband to be murdered nor did she expect she would wind up being an integral part of an assassination conspiracy against the president of both her country and the president of the United States. Not the kind of life a liaison officer was ever trained for. She was never supposed to be an active field agent.

Lucas stood and stepped across the cabin and sat down beside her, wrapping his arm around her shoulders and pulling her close to him. Elena placed her hand on his chest as she snuggled into him. She closed her eyes, praying she would not again see

Nikolai, taking from Lucas his strength and heat. The dream had cooled her body. Now, she began to thaw. She breathed in Lucas's scent and immediately felt safe. She savored the moment. The feeling of contentment and joy, not knowing when she would feel this way again. Perhaps Dmitry was right and she was keeping her head in the sand.

"Have you ever been married?" she asked after a few minutes of silence.

Why had she asked that? It was none of her business. Why should it matter to her if he had been married before or married now? Please God, don't let him be married. She hadn't spotted a wedding ring or a tan line on his finger so she guessed he wasn't. But who knew, maybe he took off his wedding band when he went on missions. She only hoped for her sanity he was single. She would hate to think she had been lusting after an attached man. It was bad enough she still felt married to Nikolai, as if she had betrayed him somehow.

She couldn't help but admit she was curious and wanted to know more about him. He was an interesting man. She hadn't known him for very long but with everything that had happened, it felt like they'd known each other forever. She was surprised she felt so comfortable with him and trusted him with her life.

She was changing. It was as though she'd been in a state of suspension these past months. Lucas was changing her, opening her eyes and showing her the world as she'd never seen it before. She wasn't sure if she'd ever be able to go back to her old life.

Is that so bad? She wondered. Did she really want to go back when she was going through life on autopilot? Never connecting or tasting the wonders the world had to offer? She forced her brain away from those thoughts. Now was not the time to be contemplating life. She'd needed to give the matter some proper thought not a rushed, emotional one decided on a train out in the middle of nowhere right before embarking on a highly dangerous mission that could get her killed.

"No," he replied.

"Ever gotten close?"

He took his time to answer. She wondered if he was deciding what to tell her and what not to tell her.

"No," he said finally. "Once the women in my life realize they can't change me and that I won't change on my own, they pack it in."

Elena frowned. "What is it they want to change about you?"

Lucas shrugged. "You'd have to ask them."

She couldn't think of anything she would change about him. But then again, she had never lived with him. The man could be a giant slob leaving discarded socks about the place and never replacing the toilet roll for all she knew. There could be a million and one things wrong with him that didn't show on the outside. Which she freely admitted was a very nice package.

"And before you ask, no, I haven't got any children."

Elena blushed. She hadn't meant to be so intrusive. She never liked delving into people's private business because she hated when people did it to her. *Time to change the subject,* she thought.

"What can we expect from Ducane?"

It was time to get back to the matter at hand. Until SAC Fitzgibbon got a hold of Alexei, they were on their own.

"A large radius explosion most likely. That's what he seems to favor. The more causalities the better. But he's a man for hire, so it'll depend on his client's specifications."

Elena nodded. "Fantastic. So how many people do you think are involved in this plot?"

"Inside or outside your government?" he asked.

"Point taken. I was just wondering if we should be worried about snipers and guns."

Lucas looked down at her, something in his eyes she didn't dare to recognize.

"Whatever happens today, Elena, know that we tried our best."

But what if our best isn't good enough?

She hated that they were alone in this. She and Lucas were both a part of great agencies. They should have had the world at their disposal. Not using aliases to purchase train tickets, slipping through back doors, and calling in favors to get their warning out. She had a notion to swap sides when this was all over.

"It's unfortunate when you can only trust two people in the entire world," she said ruefully.

"I assume one of them is me?"

She nodded. "Yes, of course."

Lucas pulled her in closer to his warm body. "That reminds me. There's a question I've been meaning to ask." He took a moment to think. "Since yesterday morning. God, has it only been a couple of days? It's seems longer, much longer. Anyway, I was going to ask you why you decided to put your trust in me."

She thought back to when she had first known she could trust him. It sort of came to her as a flash. One minute she had been uncertain, and the next she knew he would protect her with everything he had. He was just that sort of man—a man like Nikolai.

"Don't take this the wrong way, but it was because you reminded me of Nikolai."

Lucas smiled. "Well then, I'll take that as a compliment."

She closed her eyes once more. "Good. You should, because it was intended to be that way."

Chapter 29

The bullet-proof car convoy pulled up in front of the Winter Palace. Alexei Dimitrovich exited the first car and stood watch as the president made his way into the palace, stopping briefly to wave at the news cameras gathered in Palace Square to film the event. Sergei Smirnov was a fit man of fifty-something and was dressed in a form fitting steel grey suit. His brown hair had been styled carefully and his Slavic face was clean shaven.

Sergei slipped inside the doors of the palace, surrounded by Alexei's men. Men who would gladly give their lives should the need arise. Men trained for any eventuality. The Palace Square was overrun by protestors voicing their objections about every UN decision since its inception. His eyes never stopped moving, scanning every angle for a sniper. He noted FSB's own snipers ready to take a shot with their rifles. Satisfied there was no imminent danger needing to be attended to, Alexei followed the president through the palace gates and then stood by the entrance. The first part of his job was done. Now he had to wait for the American president and have a few quick words with the Secret Service.

The dogs were out, sniffing the exterior for explosives. Another agent was carrying a portable metal detector and was diligently searching for hidden weapons, leaving no place unchecked. The interior of the palace had already been swept prior to the president arriving and would continuously be done throughout the meeting. The palace had been closed to tourists for the past week to accommodate for the UN meeting.

He watched from inside as the protestors tried to push past the police barriers. *Fucking fantastic*, he thought. It might as well have been *Cirque du Soleil* with the crowds. It was going to make his job so much harder. He spoke briefly into his radio. His fellow agents replied to let him know their checkpoints were secure. *So far, so good.* He would be happy once this was all over.

He felt his phone vibrate and retrieved it from his pocket, frowning as he read the international number on the display. He flipped it open and spoke, "*Privyet.*"

Chapter 30

Michael Ducane stopped behind a thick hedge and listened as a guard announced into his radio that checkpoint four was clear. He knew from his employer's instructions that this was one of his men and the guard would ensure his safe delivery inside the structure. So far he had encountered very few problems and had, for the most part, found his designated route unguarded. He knew this was his employer's doing, directing his men to other sections of the garden when he was due to cross from one checkpoint to another.

He heard the crackle of the radio as checkpoint five declared themselves clear and stepped out from behind the hedge. The guard surveyed him from head to foot, most likely checking that he'd gotten the borrowed uniform on right and would not be questioned should someone come upon him. He nodded sharply, obviously having passed inspection. The guard shifted the rifle in his arms, allowing the long thin barrel to rest over his left arm while his right hand remained close to the trigger.

The guard began walking confidently towards the palace and Michael fell into step behind him, his olive green duffel bag hooked over one shoulder and resting on his back. He froze briefly when another guard turned the corner of the building where he had been hidden until that moment, a large German Shepherd trotting beside him, his snout to the ground. The dog looked up, locking eyes with him before continuing his task of sniffing. He wondered why, since the dog hadn't been able to detect the explosive residue on his body or even in his bag. He didn't particularly care but had to admit he was curious as to what had been done to the dogs.

The two guards didn't exchange words nor did they nod at each other in acknowledgement as they walked past each other. They both had jobs to do and apparently neither felt the need to stop for a chat in the cold. Barely a minute later, the guard and his dog had disappeared out of sight and his heartbeat slowly returned to normal. He was not used to infiltrating such heavy security and feared he would be caught at any time before he had a chance to watch the place blow. But he had to have faith in his employer, he reminded himself. He had yet to disappoint and he doubted the man would've gone to so much trouble for everything to fall to pieces at the last minute.

With renewed assurance he picked up his speed, listening as the snow crunched beneath his polished work boots. Beside him, the guard surveyed the landscape and the odd squawk of the radio mixed with the sounds of their combined breathing was the only noise. In the distance, he could just make out the screams of the protestors coming from the front of the palace.

The guard stopped at the well-hidden basement entrance. Had the guard not been there, he would've missed it and blown the whole plan. A moment later, the guard revealed a keypad on the side of the building and promptly entered the six digit code, the LED light changing from red to green.

He stepped forward and opened the heavy steel door before closing it soundlessly behind him, leaving the guard to his rounds. He quickly dusted off his boots, ensuring he left no sign he had been there and walked along the concrete encasement towards the hidden opening leading to the escape tunnels beneath the palace. The blueprints he had obtained were extremely detailed and helpful. He opened the door, the silence telling him it had been oiled recently. His benefactor had been here, and he was again pleased that his job was running so smoothly. He'd had very few jobs that had been this well-orchestrated. His employer sure had some mad organizational skills. Nothing had been left to chance.

Using his memory, he continued on towards the west side of the building, moving through the underground tunnels to St. George's Hall. He had plenty of time to plant the charges and be gone by the time the meeting was in full swing. The US president would arrive in twenty minutes and would join the Russian to enter the hall together just moments before the UN Summit was to begin. It would be one for the history books, and it would certainly finish with a bang.

Chapter 31

Lucas and Elena disembarked at St. Petersburg's Moskovsky Station and hit the ground running. The sky had darkened rapidly but he was thankful the snow had stopped falling and now only coated the ground. Elena slipped as she moved quickly over the wet sludge but managed to remain upright, her shoes not having sufficient grip for such an exercise. They pushed past the tired and irritable commuters, hearing a few choice phrases he pretended not to notice and made it to the street. Elena glanced about and frowned.

"What are you thinking?" he asked as she put her hands on her hips.

"I'm thinking that the president's life is in danger. I've been shot at and chased by my own people. I am currently on the run and will most likely be fired for insubordination not to mention potential jail time. I've just about had enough."

She reached into her purse, pulled out her SVR identification, and ran in front of the first car that was about to drive by. Unfortunately, it happened to be a red Smart car.

"You have got to be kidding," he muttered when he saw the motorist come to a stop.

Elena ignored him and flashed her identification at the driver who clearly did not like the interruption. She glared at the round man with dark facial hair who resembled a very unhappy Russian Santa Claus. "SVR. I need to borrow your car. Move it."

SVR seemed to be the magic word around here. The driver scrambled out of his vehicle as fast as his heavy-set body would allow, and Elena replaced him behind the wheel of the car and patiently waited for Lucas to hop in the passenger side. His knees dug into his stomach as he sat down in the tiny space allowed for passengers. Elena waited no longer and took off down the street weaving in and out of traffic. He watched wide-eyed as they almost got struck a couple times as she cut the other motorists off. He shook his head. And she thought *his* driving was bad.

Women drivers, he thought but was thankful when Elena had the car speeding down a narrow street and crossing over the river in no time. She hit the brake hard as they came to a mass crowd of pedestrians. He placed the palm of his hand on the dashboard in an effort to stop his head from hitting the inconvenient windshield.

He looked over at Elena. "So what's the plan?"

Elena gnawed at her bottom lip as she thought of what to do next. They were rapidly running out of time.

"Get to the Summit, get the presidents out of

harm's way, and find Ducane," she recited out loud.

Lucas nodded. "Any idea how we're going to do that?"

"No, not one," she admitted before honking the horn. When that didn't help, she gunned the engine, the crowd parting like the Red Sea to get out of her way. She pressed down hard on the accelerator and the car zoomed forward, many of the public literally diving out of the way to avoid being hit. He thought for a second that she had lost it and was actually going out of her way to attempt to run the people down but she did make a last ditch effort to swerve and narrowly avoided two men who took offense to almost being run over.

She turned into the square in front of the palace, dodging two uniformed MVD police officers who shouted and cursed at them before navigating through the protestors and narrowly missed crashing into the hundred and fifty-five foot tall column which stood proudly in the center of the square.

"Looks like the rest is on foot," she stated calmly.

Lucas bent down to the bag he had dumped in the foot well, unzipped it and removed the two weapons. He handed the Desert Eagle to Elena.

"Here. In case you need it."

Elena nodded and shoved the gun into the pocket of her coat as she got out of the car. He followed suit, the car door scraping the side of the column as he climbed out. He spared a glance at the red granite engravings on the pedestal of the column. An engraving read 'Peace and Victory' and he thought it quite fitting considering their current predicament.

He followed Elena into the sea of people. He could see the pale mint and white rectangular palace in the short distance which he'd learned on the train had been the official residence of the royal family until 1917 when the revolution broke out. Several lights lit up the palace and he could see the amazing beauty of it. The building was quite spectacular and took his breath away.

He followed Elena to the barrier separating the palace from the protestors and when she tried to hop over, a police officer in his pressed red and blue uniform came over, stopping her none too gently, pushing her back from the temporary fence. He stepped forward, ready for a battle. Elena placed a hand on his arm, silently asking him to let it go even as she glared at the MDV officer while shoving her identification in his face with her free hand.

"No unauthorized people are allowed inside," he replied.

"SVR," Elena said.

The guard repeated himself and Elena scowled at him, her face darkening as a storm brewed beneath the surface. Her eyes lit up as her gaze flicked over the palace entrance.

"Alexei, Alexei!" she yelled over top of the mass of voices threatening to drown hers out.

He followed her line of vision as she waved madly to get the attention of the tall man who was currently on his cell phone. He watched as the man, presumably Alexei, turned and sought out the origin of his name. His gaze wandered over to Elena and he held up his hand, letting her know he saw her.

"Oh, thank God," Elena said as Alexei headed over to them, his badge and special pass displayed proudly on his brown suit.

"Elena?" he said, although it came out more like a question. "Let them through," he told the officer in a tone that dared him to argue. Lucas doubted very few people ever did.

Elena jumped over the barrier and he followed. The Russian held out his hand to her and she took it, allowing him to assist her. They began moving away from the crowd and back towards the palace. Alexei's face was full of concern as he asked, "What are you doing here? The entire SVR is out looking for you."

She took a deep breath. "Tell me a man by the name of James Fitzgibbon got hold of you?"

They made their way through the gates marking the entrance to the palace. The gilded emblems of Imperial Russia glowed as a beam of light hit them. Alexei led them through the halls and turned right, heading to the eastern side of the palace.

Alexei nodded. "I just got off the phone with him." He held up his cell phone. "At first I thought it was a prank but when he mentioned you and Nikolai, I had to take him at his word. I've already radioed for back up and closed the exits. The presidents are getting to safety as we speak."

"I can't tell you how relieved I am to hear that, Alexei." She turned to Lucas. "Finally, something is going right."

He smiled at her, his hand going to her waist propelling her forward. The Russian noted the position of his hand. Lucas caught the man's eyes and wondered if he was going to comment. He didn't.

Elena glanced up, her eyebrow rising when she discovered he and the Russian sizing each other up. He bit back a chuckle as she rolled her eyes and could only imagine the words 'spare me' in her head. She made the introductions.

"Alexei Dimitrovich, this is Lucas Gates, CIA. Alexei is FSB. You didn't use your escape plans, did you? He'll be expecting that."

Alexei frowned. "Who is he?"

Lucas spoke. "Michael Ducane."

Alexei scoffed. "Of course, a bloody American."

"Alexei," Elena scolded, and the Russian had the grace to look apologetic. "Do you know a man named Igor Zimtovich?"

Alexei looked taken back. "Of course. He was the liaison officer between SVR and FSB. Why?"

"He was the one who provided Ducane with the intel."

Alexei swore under his breath.

"Yeah."

They continued moving quickly through the palace, cutting through a hall. "The UN Summit was supposed be in St. George's Hall down there." He indicated to the left as they walked past what were once apartments reserved for guests of the highest ranks. Lucas reading the information on a panel as they passed by. "Let's go down below," Alexei decided. "If this Ducane knows the layout of the palace, he would most likely hide there where the president's escape route was."

He and Elena followed Alexei down a set of

stairs hidden behind a large Peter Paul Rubens painting at the end of the hall into a tight narrow tunnel. It was lighted by one naked bulb every few feet but the light still cast shadows along the walls. She widened her eyes.

Alexei seemed to catch the surprise on Elena's face and explained. "After the assassination attempt on Alexander the Second's life in 1880, the Czar ordered the escape tunnels built in case of another attempt but never had a chance to use them. The existence of the tunnels was until recently only known by members of the royal family."

"How far do these tunnels go?" Lucas asked, looking about the meter and a half wide tunnel.

"All over. There are several hidden passageways throughout the palace. One leading to the New Hermitage and another under Palace Square. After Alexander the Third's coronation he moved his family to Gatchina Palace after his advisors told him it was impossible to secure the palace, so they were never used."

"Until now."

They continued on in silence, each in their own thoughts.

"What is his motive?" Alexei asked after some time.

"Ducane is merely a puppet," Lucas explained. "A man for hire. Your problem is whoever is footing the bills."

"And who exactly is that?"

Lucas shrugged. "That is so far undetermined."

"Whoever it is has a real taste for anarchy," Elena said. "If he'd been able to pull this off, it would've been the biggest political statement of the century. Two presidents, two countries, and potentially one big fucking war. Can you imagine what the United States would do if their president was killed in our country? It would destroy the peace between the two countries and set us back years in negotiations and trust."

Alexei's face changed. "She's right about that."

In the next minute he raised his arm and brought the butt of his gun down over her temple.

Chapter 32

It all happened so fast Lucas had no time to react. Before he could go on the attack, Dimitrovich had his pistol pointed at Lucas's heart. "Don't try it. Drop the gun."

Son-of-a-bitch, Lucas thought. The traitorous bastard. They had been wrong to involve him. They'd trusted the wrong man just like Nikolai had, and now they were going to end up like Nikolai too.

"Turn around," Alexei ordered.

He did as he was told, buying time. Maybe it wasn't over yet. He'd been in some sticky situations in the past and sometimes all it took was one moment. "So you were the traitor inside Russian Intelligence?"

He already knew the truth but he wanted the admission. His mind was working a mile a minute while he tried to think of a way to get free. He had no doubt that Dimitrovich had lied to them about having moved the presidents. No, they were where they were supposed to be and if he didn't come up with a plan, both of them would be dead along with him and Elena and many others.

"You know, you're actually helping me out," Alexei said as he patted Lucas down, discovering his weapon and pocketing it along with the spare magazine. "When all this is done and they find your body amongst the others, questions will arise. Had the Americans had foreknowledge? Was it a CIA sanctioned hit? This act of terrorism will be instrumental in the destroying US-Russian relations."

He looked down at Elena's crumpled form and saw blood matting her hair in the pale light. He clenched his palms into tight fists, feeling unbelievably useless and a complete failure. He had promised Dmitry he would take care of Elena. He was breaking that promise.

Dimitrovich followed his gaze for a second then turned his full attention back to Lucas. "Don't worry about Elena. I'll take good care of her. Until I don't need her anymore, of course."

Lucas could feel the rage burning inside him. If this bastard touched one hair on Elena's head he was going to rip him limb from limb. Diplomatic relations be damned.

"Let's go." Using the barrel of the gun, Alexei prodded Lucas forward, directing him where he wanted Lucas to go. They went down several more tunnels before coming to an opening. The Russian pushed him into the room recently carved out of the concrete. Michael Ducane stood high on a ladder, his hands reaching towards the ceiling as he pressed the compliant C4 into the concrete.

"About fucking time," he muttered loudly as he

spotted Alexei coming towards him.

"Is there a problem?"

Ducane's eyebrow rose as he took in Lucas. "You tell me."

"Nothing that concerns you. Are you almost done?"

"Ten more minutes and I'll be on my way."

"Can you speed things up? I have some other matters to attend to."

Lucas knew the man was speaking about Elena, who would soon regain consciousness.

Ducane grunted and returned his focus to the dark grey square. "I'm not exactly baking a cake here, you know."

He retrieved some wires from a tool box precariously balanced on the top step and imbedded the wire.

"Just do your job, Ducane."

Above them, Lucas heard the sounds of a man talking into a microphone. He could just make out the words: "*Introducing the President of the Russian Federation, Sergei Smirnov.*"

Lucas went cold. They were directly under St. George's Hall. This is what they had planned all along. This was why Nagregor had uploaded the blueprints for the Winter Palace. He watched as Ducane attached two wires to the small electronic timer. It was getting too real.

He thought of the men above them, the men trying to make the world a better place, and here he was standing beside two men who wanted to destroy that.

Not while I'm still alive.

He elbowed Alexei. The man, unprepared for the attack, dropped his gun and lost his balance, falling to the cold, hard floor. Lucas didn't wait to watch him land. He took off down the labyrinth of passageways beneath the palace. He heard the Russian yell at Ducane to stop him.

Lucas could hear Ducane's footsteps behind him as he navigated the halls. He was at a distinct disadvantage not having had time to peruse the schematics of the structure. Ducane came up behind him and tackled him. They both went down and rolled about the concrete floor. Lucas used his strength to push Ducane away so that his fist could connect with the man's jaw before untangling himself and finding the exit out of the tunnels and into St. George's Hall.

"Bomb. Evacuate. Bomb. Evacuate!" he yelled at the room. The Secret Service were immediately on the president, pulling him away to safety. Ducane followed him into the room and produced a gun. He raised it up and took a shot at Lucas. He hit the floor hard. Several screams of terror filled the room and the diplomats began to panic, pushing at each other so they could escape, some being knocked over in an effort to get out. Lucas thought fleetingly about the irony of the situation. Apparently diplomatic relations go out the window when their own lives are in jeopardy.

"Gun!" was shouted by one of the agents.

The Secret Service and FSB agents all brought out their weapons in a practiced movement within seconds from the moment Ducane's gun was spotted. Every gun was trained towards the door where Ducane stood. Because of the panicking accumulation of people, no agent had a clear shot and couldn't risk shooting the bystanders. Each set of eyes were ever vigilant, moving restlessly around the room, assessing for danger.

The large double doors at the entrance to St George's Hall closed shut, locking the occupants of the room inside.

He shouted at the Secret Service and FSB agents. "CIA—get them out of here!" He grabbed hold of an agent as he moved by. "Don't take the escape route, it's been compromised."

The agent studied Lucas, presumably judging his character before nodding. Lucas passed the test. The agent moved back to join his team, relaying the information.

Chapter 33

Elena felt something digging into her hip and sat up. She heard an incessant ringing echoing in her head, causing it to throb more painfully. Her skull felt like it had been split in two. She reached up and touched her head, feeling a damp stickiness. She glanced at her hand, not surprised to see blood on her fingertips. It explained the nausea. Where was she? How did she get here? Slowly the events came back to her. Alexei had struck her with something, most likely his gun. He had been involved from the start? Whenever that may have been. She had never picked him for anything but a patriot. The betrayal cut deep. He'd been planning this day for over six months, all the while lying to her face about how he cared. Was that why he had shown up at her office a few days ago, pumping her for information. She hadn't given him anything but still she felt used. She had trusted him. Nikolai had trusted him.

She got to her feet slowly and held onto the wall as her head swam, the tunnel whirling around her. She probably had a concussion. She quickly ran her hands down from her waist and over her hips and felt the bulge of the Desert Eagle Lucas had obtained from Iosif. She yanked it out of her pocket as she made her way towards the screaming voices, her mind flashing back to the basic weapons training every agent, liaison officer, and paper pusher employed by SVR had to complete. She took the safety off and then replaced it, reacquainting herself with the powerful weapon.

She retraced her steps. She hadn't been paying much attention on the way down but she managed to navigate the maze of hallways back to the hidden door at the end of the corridor near the apartments. She turned right, cutting through the Grand Church and Guard Room and ran down the antechamber making up the Military Gallery, before stopping outside St. George's Hall. The fire doors had been rigged to close, trapping them all inside.

Not wanting to waste bullets or accidentally shoot someone inside the room, she stuffed the Desert Eagle inside the waistband of her borrowed jeans and went in search of something to jimmy the door. She hit the jackpot when she found an antiquated axe hanging from the wall, most likely dating back to Catherine the Great. Without any qualms over the fact the axe was a piece of history, she yanked it off the wall and took it back to the large heavy wood double doors. She was glad Carey wasn't here to witness her lack of regard to the antiques inside the palace. Her friend would probably have a heart attack to see the artifacts treated so carelessly. She raised the axe high and started hacking away at the centuries old door.

They don't make doors the way they used to, she thought as she kept on chopping, barely making a dent in the wood. Her arms screamed as she raised the axe again and again. She concentrated on the doorknob and lock, and after a few more hard whacks, the lock broke off with the knob and the door opened, diplomats spilling out, almost knocking her down.

There's gratitude for you.

She weaved through the frightened civil servants who were making hasty getaways and searched for Lucas. He had to be here somewhere. She spotted the FSB agents and the Secret Service coming towards her with the two presidents in tow. The agents all had their guns drawn and directed them at anyone who came too close.

Elena pulled aside an agent of the Secret Service and handed him the axe. She flashed her identification in front of his eyes.

"Be careful, that door was rigged. We have a breach in security among our agency and the FSB. Vital information has been passed on. If a man named Alexei Dimitrovich with the FSB approaches, you're well within your rights to shoot to kill. Cross over into the Armorial Hall straight through there. That will lead you to the Court Garden."

She then told him the easiest way to safety: cut through the west side of the palace, past the private rooms that once belonged to the Imperial family to the West Garden where the government cars could pick up the presidents, taking them out of sight and away from the protestors.

The agent nodded enthusiastically before proceeding out the door into the elaborately designed room. She didn't wait to see if the agent took her advice. Instead she entered the hall, gun at ready.

Chapter 34

Lucas glanced about the room, the mass of people finally thinning. Who knew when the bomb below would go off, or rather when Dimitrovich would make it go off? He still had to get to Elena and move her to safety before going after the traitorous bastard. It wasn't his country that had been betrayed but still felt outraged on the offended country's behalf.

St. George's Hall was a beautiful room. Once the principal throne room, it had tall, white colonnades lining each side of the room, leading up towards where the throne would be on a platform at the end of the Hall, had it not been removed to be replaced with a podium and microphone. Behind the Hall was Apollo Hall which connected the palace with the Small Hermitage.

The hall had been divided into two sides, left and right with long banquet tables, covered in a white damask tablecloth. Each spot at the table was marked with a nameplate that had the name of the nation the delegate was from.

Lucas spotted Ducane coming at him and turned to deflect the fist. Ducane wasn't mucking about, his fists, his feet all going for the most sensitive body parts. Lucas did the same, his fist connecting with Ducane's nose and he heard the satisfying crunch. Blood poured from his nose. Ducane pulled the gun from his waistband and squeezed the trigger. Lucas dove for safety even as the bullet ripped through his shoulder. He fell to the floor, cutting his hands on broken glass. His shoulder burned like fire. He pulled a few pieces of errant glass out of his skin. Blood welled at each cut and his coat was already damp from his shoulder. He was losing blood fast.

Ducane stepped closer, the gun in his hand steady as he moved around the overturned table that was protecting Lucas and aimed his shot to kill. Lucas had no time to evade him and realized with clarity that he was done. His life over. His mind filled with his regrets. Thoughts of Elena bounced around his head and he wished he'd had a chance to tell her how he felt. He heard the shot echo through the Hall and for a second thought he'd been shot again. But when no new pain followed he looked up at Ducane, a neat hole in his head, blood dribbling out as he fell to the floor.

He watched with appreciation as Elena approached, the Desert Eagle in her hand. She seemed unaffected by the fact she had just killed someone, but then again the shock mightn't have worn off yet and she would most probably break down later.

"Where's Alexei?" she asked, her gaze moving

restlessly around the room. He could see the guilt in her eyes and knew she blamed herself. If she hadn't told Fitzgibbon to warn Dimitrovich, they might have prevented this situation. She looked down at him and saw the blood soaking through his jacket. She paled, her eyes widening.

"Lucas, you're hurt!"

He was touched by her concern. He had never had a woman concerned about him like that before. He certainly hadn't had one shoot someone to protect him, either. It left him feeling strange or perhaps that was the loss of blood. Out of the corner of his eye, he saw Dimitrovich. The Russian's face was contorted with rage, his weapon in his hand. He raised his gun and pointed it at Elena.

"Elena!"

Lucas reached up and grabbed hold of her wrist and yanked her to the floor beside him as Dimitrovich squeezed the trigger. The bullet whizzed above their heads, coming to a stop when it hit the wall behind them. The sound of the gun discharging echoed through the hall, piercing his eardrums. He didn't have time to ask her if she was okay. Since she was still moving and hadn't said anything, he assumed she was.

Alexei glanced at his watch. "Any second now."

He and Elena shared a look before he wrapped his good arm around her waist and rolled her under him. He barely had time to register how good her body felt beneath his before the ground below them began to shake. A loud groan reverberated through the room as the explosive converted into gas. The pressure caused a shockwave that rose up making the C4 discharge beneath them. Lucas prayed for a little luck as the floor above the device was torn up, bits of concrete and flooring flying in all directions from the velocity of the detonation.

Lucas kept Elena covered with his body, a hand covering his head for protection. She was tense beneath him, her fingers digging into his coat.

He watched helplessly as several delegates and their guards unfortunately hiding on the platform directly above the bomb were thrown up into the air, pieces of their bodies hitting the roof. A hole was ripped through the wall behind the platform and the podium was catapulted into the small Apollo Hall. Large chunks of the concrete flooring were thrown through the exterior wall and out into the snow. Fires broke out around the point of impact and furniture exploded nearby, scattering the pieces to the far reaches of the room. The screams of panic and fear from the frightened delegates were barely audible over the ringing in his ears.

Tables were overturned by the force of the blast and one nearby exploded, a piece striking the crown of his head. Stars burst in his vision as he felt the blow. He could feel the resulting pounding and the trickle of warm blood right before the impact rendered him unconscious.

Chapter 35

Dust and debris began to settle. The fire raged, threatening to spread. The smell of death and smoke lingered in the air. Elena coughed, her hand a fist crumpling Lucas's coat. Her heart pounded in her chest and she struggled to breathe, hindered by the hundred and eighty pound or so man crushing her into the floor.

"Lucas," she said, not hearing her voice as she spoke. The bomb blast had shot her hearing, a constant ringing in her ear. Luckily her eardrum had not burst from the impact on her senses. Her mouth was dry and her throat was raw, probably due to the smoke and dust she was inhaling. She needed water. Slowly she began to hear the distant wail of a siren as several fire engines approached, the sound contorting painfully in her ear but there was no disguising the well-known sound of help on the way. They would need to get here quick and diffuse the fire before it had a chance to spread to the rest of the palace. It would take emergency crews a while to sort through the debris and body parts. The bomb had been planted directly under the platform at the end of the room where the presidents would surely have been had Lucas not warned them.

She tried to move, nudging Lucas. She was worried he hadn't made it and was immensely relieved when she felt him move above her. She gently rolled him off her body and saw the goose egg appearing on his head where a bit of wood had hit him. She sat up, looking around at the sight as she did. The once beautiful state room had been destroyed.

She felt something cold against her head and heard the unmistakable sound of a gun being cocked through the cotton in her ears. She went still, her pounding heart suddenly stopping and she instantly went cold. A hand reached down and yanked her to her feet.

"Alexei?"

"Put your hands behind your back."

His mouth was practically on her ear as he spoke. She shivered and wondered what happened to the Desert Eagle. Where had she dropped it? She did as he asked and put her hands behind her back. He roughly brought her wrists together and she felt the cool steel of his handcuffs connect around each wrist. How the hell would she get out of this? She glanced down at Lucas who unfortunately remained unconscious.

Please Lucas, she begged. *Wake up.*

He didn't. Time for a new plan. She tried to think of one, looking about the room for a weapon. Not that it would do her any good now that her hands were bound behind her back. Elena cursed the turn of events. She would have to go along with him until he was distracted and then she would run.

Alexei half carried, half dragged her out of the room. She stumbled a few times over debris as she tried to keep up with his long strides. He immediately reached out and righted her each time, his hand remaining like a vice on her arm.

Chapter 36

Lucas's head swam as he rose to his feet. His head pounded like a jackhammer and he could've done with a bottle full of Vicodin and several glasses of Scotch. His shoulder throbbed as he moved his arm and he gritted his teeth against the searing pain. His mind tried to make sense of the images surrounding his vision. Firefighters barged into the hall with their hoses at the ready, the water spraying over the flames. He watched as medics entered with their medical bags and moved over to the visible bodies lying scattered about the hall. His memory came rushing back and he immediately sought out Elena. If anything happened to her he would never forgive himself.

"Do you destroy everything you touch?" Mishkin demanded, as he appeared beside him, his round face red.

The words started off garbled but by the time he was done speaking the constant ringing had lessened and Lucas could once again hear other sounds. He wasn't sure that was a good thing if he was about to get a lecture from Mishkin. Lucas ran the fingers of his good arm through his hair as he took in the damage.

Oops.

He had meant to diffuse the bomb but having unsuccessfully accomplished that, had done the next best thing and called for an evacuation. He could understand Mishkin's anger. He would feel the same if someone failed to prevent a disaster at the White House.

"Mishkin, are the presidents safe?" he croaked out as if he hadn't used his voice in a while. How long had it been since the bomb went off? How long had he been unconscious and where the hell was Elena? He remembered rolling her beneath him for protection. She should have still been there when he recovered. Had she, finding him unconscious, gone for help or had something else happened to her?

"A few cuts here and bruises there but they will live to tell about it, thanks to you. Our country is in debt to you."

Lucas nodded. Good to know. One crisis adverted, or rather two. Hopefully that meant he was no longer a wanted man. He caught the fleeting glimpse of Dimitrovich and Elena exiting through a hidden door at the other side of the room out the corner of his eye, *son-of-a-goddamn-bitch*.

"Good. Give me your gun."

He had expected Mishkin to protest. Instead, the director passed over the Russian Federation's Government issued pistol.

"May I ask as to why?" he politely enquired as if Lucas was merely asking to borrow a pen.

"I have something to do. I'll see you later."
He ran after Elena.

Chapter 37

Alexei pushed her down a hall and to the ground when he came to a dead end, a steel blast door blocking their exit. After going through the hidden escape door in St. George's Hall, Alexei had pulled her down a narrow staircase that had led to the basement and back into the hidden tunnels under the palace. Adrenaline pumped through her, the only thing keeping her moving. She was exhausted. It had been a long few days. She had tripped a few more times on the way since her arms were behind her back and she had no way to balance herself as she and Alexei made a swift getaway. She wasn't exactly sure of his plan but knew she was his insurance. There was no other viable reason to keep her with him.

She was fuming. She had trusted this man, confided in him. She had gone past scared and annoyed to downright pissed off. She didn't plan on making this easy for him. Certainly not let him use her to make his escape. He was a traitor to his country and of his friendship with Nikolai. The latter pissed her off the most.

It all made sense to her now. Nikolai had called on Alexei when he had discovered the plot. He knew it went high within the ranks of the government and was unsure who to trust. He had sorely misjudged his friendship with Alexei and had paid the price.

"It was you who provided the intel to Ducane, wasn't it? Zimtovich just worked for you." He grunted and she took that as assent. "So this was your big plan all along? This is why you killed Nikolai?"

And she knew it was him—personally *him*. Nikolai trusted him as she had. They had been friends since the academy, had been his best man at his wedding. The amount of times he had come to dinner, then worked on a case with Nikolai while they drank Vodka together. She felt sick, sick with grief, sick with anger, sick at herself for believing his lies.

"He trusted the wrong person," Alexei said simply.

All those years of friendship had meant nothing to him. The bastard had waited for Nikolai in their apartment. She remembered Nikolai giving him a key. She could see him waiting in the dark, listening to the key in the door as Nikolai unlocked it and entered their home, waiting for him to come closer, revealing himself as 'the friend' before taking Nikolai's life away.

One thing made Elena smile. Nikolai had outsmarted him, had not fully trusted the man he had known for years. It must have been frustrating for Alexei, being unable to find his carefully laid plans. After searching the apartment and realizing they weren't there, how he must have sweated. Worried that Nikolai had passed them on to Vladimir after it became apparent she had known nothing about them.

He had not guessed that Nikolai had made a copy of her wedding ring and had swapped them out one night while she had slept. Nikolai had the last laugh and she imagined him sticking it to Alexei from the grave.

"Why? What is this all about? Your hatred of anything besides Russia?"

"At first, yes, but then I found our president to be a spineless coward. Unable to stand up for what is best for this country, *our* country. He doesn't deserve to be called our president. It is time for a new president."

Her eyes widened. "You wanted to kill Sergei Smirnov just so his opponent would become President? Was he in on this with you? Is that how far this goes?"

"Smirnov should never have been made president. He is a weakling. Yuri Volstov was always the better man."

She wasn't any better off knowing his motive. Nothing could explain his actions in her eyes. She imagined the sequence of events, Nikolai's death, arranging for Ducane to slip through immigration and get in touch with Alvin Pochenchov. All for a man like Yuri Volstov. There was a reason Yuri failed in the polls. His plan for Russia was barely two steps away from another communist regime.

"And a raving psychotic," she said.

Alexei slapped her across the mouth, splitting her lip and snapping her head back. She fell to the concrete floor and tasted blood in her mouth right before he grabbed her hard, bruising her soft flesh as he brought her to her feet and through the blast door he'd just opened. She bit her bottom lip, determined not to cry out in pain and give him any satisfaction.

"So help me, Alexei, I will kill you."

His thin restraint snapped and he pushed her head first against the wall. She was dazed as her head connected with the bricks. She blinked to clear her vision. Alexei turned her around slowly, keeping her against the wall, unable to move away from him. His face close to hers. She felt the skin on her hands tear as they scraped against the rough surface of the wall where he kept her pinned.

"Really? From where I'm standing, you're the dead one. Well, at least not until I get out of here anyway."

She spat at him. "You bastard."

She struggled with him, surprising him. Her knee came up and connected with his groin. He doubled over in pain, dropping to his knees, holding his family jewels in one hand, and grabbing her ankle in the other as she tried to get away. She kicked at him with her free leg, her thick leather shoes connecting with his ribs, his face, anywhere she could get at him and felt immense satisfaction at the sound of his ribs cracking under the pressure. Her foot rammed his protecting hand into his bruised genitals and his face paled. He released her and she

229

took off running in the direction he had been taking her, deciding not to turn back with him still there.

She didn't know where she was or where she was going. She only knew she had to get as far away from Alexei as possible. If only she could find the exit and get topside, the area would certainly be crawling with emergency personnel.

She stopped when she got to a small circular room with five tunnels spouting out in different directions. She would have to choose. Which one was freedom? Would all of them take her away from this place? Away from Alexei? She quickly made her decision. She'd just stepped forward into the tunnel of her choice when she was grabbed from behind as Alexei emerged from another tunnel. She struggled with him, causing him to lose balance and he backhanded her across the face, stunning her into submission. Tears burned in her eyes, once for the slap, the second because she had failed in getting away from him.

Alexei dragged her down the tunnel she had planned on going down. Cold water appeared on the floor as it leaked through several cracks in the concrete. As they made their way deeper into the tunnel the water rose to ankle depth, seeping into her socks and chilling her feet. Alexei pushed her to the ground once again. She landed in the freezing water, soaking her jeans as he opened another blast door to reveal the frigid air outside. He got her to her feet and through the darkness she could just make out a white, thirty-four foot Sport Cabin resting on the choppy water of the river Neva.

Alexei pulled her towards the boat and knew that

was his destination. She glanced frantically around and found nobody. They were alone. She assumed any locals were watching the drama unfold behind her at the palace and she realized she and Alexei had completely passed beneath the palace and the embankment dividing the palace and the river.

Elena began to panic. She was handcuffed, alone with a murderer who had no reservations about killing her. She struggled, fighting Alexei with everything she possessed as he continued toward the boat, undaunted by her attempts. With one last effort to free herself, Elena let her feet drag, making him pull her full weight.

Realizing she was no longer cooperating with him, Alexei turned and picked her up, draping her over his shoulder like a sack of flour. She tried to kick at him, but he dodged each attempt.

He hopped into the boat and dumped her unceremoniously onto the deck, stepping over her to turn on the engine and prepare to take the boat out.

Elena gritted her teeth at the shooting pain attacking her body from the impact of landing on the hard deck. Tears escaped her eyes, rolling down her cool cheeks only to freeze halfway down. The night's temperature had dropped well under the record low and Elena knew all Alexei had to do was drop her overboard into the river and she would either freeze to death or drown as her winter clothes became waterlogged and pulled her down beneath the surface.

Do something, you idiot, she chastised herself. *If you die, it's no one's fault but your own. So get up and do something now before it's too late.*

Chapter 38

Lucas pushed open the blast door and smelled the river. He looked out into the black and white coastline illuminated by the full moon above to see Dimitrovich standing at the helm of a Sport Cabin and he heard the engine catch. He was almost too late. He started running across the snow covered ramp, reaching out to the small dock boats could moor on. He almost lost his footing a few times but managed to remain on his feet.

He had to get to Elena and stop Alexei from escaping. If Alexei managed to escape him now, it would prove more than difficult to catch up to him. The Sport Cabin being the only powerboat he could see that was docked on this side of the river. He had no idea how one would go about arranging a boat block farther up the river. Did they even have a coastguard here? He pulled Mishkin's pistol from his waistband and took the safety off. He had no doubt whatsoever that he would need it. His assumption was proven correct when he saw two men come out from the cabin. Neither appeared happy to be there and both had the hired mercenary look. He didn't like the fact that Elena was alone on the boat with them. He knew what those types could and would do if the price was right. He pushed himself to run faster, the cold air biting into his skin.

Only a little bit farther.

He watched as the two men stopped in their tracks and took stock of the woman lying helplessly on the deck before looking to their employer for instructions.

"Untie the boat," Lucas heard Alexei bark.

The burly first man walked over the bow of the boat and reached out, untying the boat's painter from around the wood stump.

"Let's get out of here."

The Russian started to steer the boat away from the embankment, just as Lucas took a running jump from the dock onto the deck. He almost missed. Another centimeter or two and he would have ended up in the river, which flowed upstream into the Gulf of Finland. He knew the temperature would be well below freezing. Any more than five minutes underwater and hypothermia set in.

"Lucas!" Elena shouted excitedly.

Alexei swung around from the small cabin as he landed hard on the deck. Swearing, he brought up his gun.

Lucas had his pistol pointed at the Russian just as the other man grabbed Elena and pointed his at her, holding her in front of his body, using her a human shield. *Talk about a Mexican standoff,* he thought.

Alexei shook his head, chastising him. "I wouldn't do that. One dead SVR agent is fine, but two? I don't think they'll like that."

Lucas took stock of his options. He didn't have many so it didn't take long. He kept his eyes on Alexei while also keeping track of the other two men. He couldn't afford to let his guard down. Not when Elena's life was on the line.

"It's over. The presidents are safe. There's nowhere to go."

"There's always a place to go," Alexei corrected.

"No place we can't find you. No place *I* can't find you," he promised, coolly.

Elena struggled, making it difficult for Alexei to keep his concentration. Her expression was mutinous and Lucas prayed Alexei didn't accidentally shoot her *or* on purpose. She stomped down hard on the man's instep before ramming her elbow as far back into his ribs as possible.

Alexei screamed out in pain and pushed Elena into Lucas who caught her as she was thrown into him but the force knocked them both off their feet. His gun flew out of his grip as his hand hit the deck, jarring him and it slid across to the port side.

Lucas was on his feet in seconds, launching himself at Alexei. His body hit the other man hard, hoping to knock him over, to gain some advantage but the man remained steady on his feet. Lucas sent a fist into Alexei's stomach, momentarily winding him. The boat made a sharp turn suddenly as one of the Russian's men took the helm. He and Alexei swayed precariously as they both tried to remain standing. The boat moved erratically from side to side on the choppy water.

Elena, who was in the process of awkwardly getting to her feet, was once more thrown onto the deck. Her head hit the side railing as she went down for the second time that night.

Lucas grabbed his opponent's right hand, twisting at the wrist and dislodging the gun from Alexei's grip. The gun went up into the air and bounced off the same railing Elena's head did just moments before and into the dark water surrounding them.

They were well away from the dock now, with nowhere to run and nowhere to hide. Seriously outnumbered and disadvantaged. Elena was no help with her hands bound behind her back and he couldn't see his weapon. He was going to shoot the man behind the wheel just on principal. He glanced around the deck for a weapon, unable to locate one, then brought up his fist and clocked Alexei.

Alexei blocked his next punch and pushed him away. The Russian then hooked his leg behind Lucas's, tripping him. Lucas reached out and grabbed Alexei's coat as he went down, bringing the other man with him. They rolled around the deck, a mass of arms and legs as they fought each other. Fists went flying, colliding with faces, arms, and torsos.

Chapter 39

Elena sat up, the cold air reviving her. She took stock of their situation. Not good. Her entire body ached and her head continued to pound. At least the ringing in her ears had dissipated to a soft whistle. Lucas and Alexei were on the deck in the midst of a fight, rolling around like a couple of boys. What looked oddly amusing was anything but and she could hear the grunts and hisses of pain as the two men fought to the death. She climbed to her feet as she watched the second man start towards Lucas, who until now, had been idly standing by enjoying the show while the first man continued to drive the boat.

That's not going to happen, comrade, she thought. Elena kicked the man hard, shoving him to the side using her shoulder, causing him to lose balance and fall overboard. She deliberately fell to her knees in an effort to remain inside the boat. She watched as the man was swallowed by the darkness, the boat leaving him behind in the freezing night.

The boat suddenly stopped veering precariously

side to side in what she assumed was an attempt to displace Lucas. The man steering the boat stepped out of his protective cabin, letting the small boat navigate itself up the river on autopilot. Elena tried to move away as he came towards her but she wasn't fast enough and he grabbed hold of her roughly. She fought him, struggling, attempting to throw him off balance with her weight. Unfortunately, she didn't have a lot to work with and her plan was unsuccessful. He grinned at her cruelly before pushing her hard towards the cabin.

She shivered at the look on his face, his thoughts well revealed. He was going to enjoy killing her. She swallowed hard as fear enveloped her, wrapping her in an immobilizing cocoon. She fought against herself, refusing defeat. If she was going to die, she was going to die fighting. She loved life too much to meekly allow this man to hurt her. She bucked wildly, using every ounce of anger and resentment whirling inside her against him. He slapped her hard, once, twice, and then a third time. She felt her cheek sting and the tears blur her vision. The man grabbed at the backs of her thighs and yanked her off her feet. She landed on her back, her hands crushed beneath her as he climbed on top of her, mounting her. She struggled against him, wiggling to escape his grasp.

She caught sight of Lucas as he caught Alexei in a choke-hold. Alexei struggled wildly, his oxygen cut off. The boat swayed precariously on the water and for a second she thought it might capsize. The waves brought the frosty water over the side of the boat and onto the deck. Lucas glanced over at her as she fought against Alexei's man. His eyes narrowed and he pushed Alexei toward the railing just as the side of the boat swayed downwards towards the water and his body disappeared beneath a wave of water.

Lucas moved quickly and yanked the second man off her before throwing him hard against the wall of the cabin.

"Are you all right?" he asked, concern in his gaze as he gave her a brief once over and despite it being a health check, warmed her immensely.

"Y-yes," she stammered, nodding, almost forgetting where they were and why as time stood still, the heat in Lucas's eyes causing her heart to beat wildly. She blinked as a light mist of river water sprayed her face and her eyes widened as Alexei reemerged from beneath a deluge of water as the boat righted itself. He let go of the railing and started towards them, his face contorted with such fury that she barely recognized him. "Lucas, watch…"

Lucas spun around too late to stop the fist from hitting him hard in the jaw, his teeth clattering together. Alexei, sensing a weak moment, reached over to Lucas's shoulder and dug his thumb into the open wound. Lucas screamed out in agony and she felt his pain acutely.

She scrunched her body into a tiny ball. Her knees against her chest as she worked her handcuffed hands under her buttocks and beneath her thighs, placing her right foot and leg in the small leeway of space between her wrists and body as she rolled onto her back. The metal of the handcuffs cut into her skin as she pulled her hands as far away as possible, making room for her to move. Blood made her wrists slippery as her skin tore with the effort to bring the handcuffs to the front of her body. After several moves which twisted and warped her body in a way any contortionist would be proud of, she managed the feat.

She stood and her gaze found Lucas. His skin was pale, almost translucent, his lips in a tight line on his face as he battled the pain.

"Dammit, Alexei, stop it," she yelled, powerless to change the outcome she inevitably saw. Her attention completely on Lucas, she had forgotten about the second man. He rose to his feet, the movement snapping her attention back. He stepped forward and grabbed her coat before she could evade him. He pulled her towards him. Her head snapped back and connected with his face. She had the pleasure of hearing his nose break. Blood spurted from his nose and his hands came up to cover it, leaving the rest of him unprotected as she used the techniques Nikolai had taught her.

Her husband had made sure she could protect herself against attackers. She thanked Nikolai silently as her knee rammed the man's balls so far up inside of him she expected them to pop out his mouth. The man screamed in pain and fell to his knees. She promptly stepped around him and hooked the chain of her handcuffs around his neck and brought his body toward her stomach. She placed her right foot on his back, pushing him away from her, effectively strangling him. He fought her as he struggled for breath but she only pulled the chain tighter around his neck. Within just a few minutes he slumped over and she withdrew. The man fell to the deck, eyes open, staring sightlessly into the night.

Elena turned to watch Lucas fall to his knees. She knew he couldn't hold up much longer. Fresh blood coated his jacket sleeve and she had no idea how much blood he had already lost. Alexei stood looking down at him, an expression of triumph on his face. She knew he was about to kill Lucas. She couldn't let that happen.

Elena, do something, she told herself, her mind blank at what she could do to help. She desperately sought a weapon, anything she could use against Alexei. The deck of the Sport Cabin was clear of clutter, the cleanest boat she had ever seen.

Her mind suddenly flashed on Lucas's gun. She remembered it had flown out of his hand and across the deck. She rapidly searched for the pistol but in the darkness it was hard to see. She heard the sound of metal scraping against wood and saw the gun slide back and forth from one side of the deck to the other, the metal catching the light from the full moon. She ran towards it, past the two men, and placed a foot on top of the pistol, effectively stopping it from sliding. She called out to Lucas before kicking the gun toward him. He reached out and in one smooth motion picked up the weapon and shot Alexei before the man had a chance to react.

Alexei's eyes widened in surprise as the bullet tore through his chest. Blood ran in dark rivulets and soaked his coat. The boat rocked dangerously and listed to one side. Alexei lost his footing and he reached out and caught hold of Lucas plunging them both overboard into the icy river.

"Die, bastard," she heard Lucas say as they hit the water.

"Lucas!" she called out. She ran into the protective cabin and over to the control panel where she slowed the knots down on the boat to an idle. She had no idea how to reverse in the small boat and didn't want to waste time trying. She radioed for help, her voice quivering from the cold. She was scared. She tried not to panic, despite knowing Lucas was going to require immediate medical attention if he was still alive. Supplies that were unlikely to be on the boat. No. Not if. He was alive, she knew it deep in her bones. He couldn't leave her. It wasn't in his nature. He was a fighter. She didn't know him well but she knew enough about his character to know he hadn't given up yet. So neither would she.

She moved back to the side of the boat, searching the surrounding inky black river for any sign of Lucas, desperately calling his name.

Chapter 40

Lucas had never been so cold in his life. He hated being cold and wondered if he was dying. He opened his eyes and found himself immersed in water, his body growing sluggish, his mind slowly shutting down. He struggled to surface, his heavy winter clothes dragging him farther under. Using his last remaining strength, the urge to see Elena safe foremost in his mind, he removed his waterlogged coat and fought his way to the surface, taking in deep breaths as he broke free. The cold stabbed at him like a thousand knives. He gritted his teeth against the pain, placing one arm in front of the other as he simultaneously kicked, making his way towards the boat idling nearby. He could hear Elena's frantic screams calling for him.

Only a little more to go, he told himself. *Then I can rest. Get to safety and everything will be all right.*

He grabbed hold of the side of the boat and tried to pull himself up. His strength rapidly waning. He felt someone grab hold of him and pull and together they heaved him up and over. He flopped down on the deck panting from the exertion.

"Are you okay?" he asked Elena when she jumped on him, tugging at his clothes.

"I've had better days," she admitted as she tossed his discarded clothes on the deck beside them. He shivered uncontrollably and vaguely noticed her handcuffed wrists were now in front of her as she yanked at his pants zipper and struggled with the damp fabric. He didn't have the energy to protest. Not that he'd ever protested against a beautiful woman in a haste to get him naked. She stripped him bare except for his boxers before laying down on top of him and rolling them into the space blanket she'd obviously found stashed onboard. She rubbed her hands up and down his arms in an effort to warm him.

His teeth chattered loudly. "Haven't we all?"

His eyelids were heavy. Elena began shaking him. He opened his eyes and glared up at her.

"God, woman, let a man have his rest," he growled. "It's been a tough couple of days."

"I know. I've been right there with you."

He felt the chill of the metal on his chest from her handcuffs. "I suppose we better get you out of them."

"We will. Soon. Just concentrate on getting warm. We can't have you getting hypothermia, now can we?" her voice broke, belying her seemingly calm composure. He fought against his uncooperative limbs in order to comfort her and lost. He'd never felt more powerless in his life and the sound of Elena swallowing back tears cut him deep.

The wail of sirens filled the night, growing louder as they neared. The sound of a motor started not too far away. "No, we can't have that. I hear sirens, can you hear them too?"

She nodded her head.

"I radioed for help while you were in the water. They should be here soon."

She held onto him tighter, snuggling into him. The warmth of her body burning his own until the pain was excruciating but he knew the agony meant he would recover, the feeling coming back into his extremities. He breathed in her scent, knowing he would never forget her smell for as long as he lived and felt her cool, soft lips against his chilled cheek.

"Hold on," she whispered, her warm breath fanning against his neck. "You have to hold on."

"I'm not going anywhere," he promised, even as he fought against his exhausted body.

"You're going to be all right. You have to be all right, Lucas," he heard her say before the darkness took him under.

Chapter 41

Ten frightening minutes later, they were back on land. Lucas had been taken away in an ambulance for treatment of his gunshot wound and for observation. It appeared as if she'd managed to slow the onset of hypothermia for which she was exceedingly thankful. It would seem he was going to pull through okay. The tightness around her heart eased somewhat with the diagnosis. Elena sat in another ambulance watching the emergency personnel move about, helping the injured and clearing debris. One of the local officers had arranged for the body of Alexei's man to be taken to the morgue. The water police were still dredging the river for Alexei himself and his second hired man. So far, neither had been found.

She had already made a brief statement and was expected to make a full one in the morning, after she rested. She figured she would be making statements for a long time coming.

The medic told her to hold still, dabbing disinfectant at one of her many cuts and grazes.

"Ouch!" she complained. Granted she only had a concussion and minor injuries, but in her mind they were just as painful and important as Lucas's. *Well, not quite*, she thought when she remembered the paleness of his skin. The blood gone from his face, the coldness of his body. The man had certainly been put through a wringer tonight. She shivered as a gust of wind blew past and pulled the blanket wrapped around her shoulders closer. She winced as she involuntarily flexed her wrists, which had begun to bruise. The medic had already disinfected the cuts made by the handcuffs and had even given her a tetanus shot after bandaging her wrists.

Director Mishkin walked towards her, stopping when he was standing over her. She assumed he got some pleasure from being able to finally look down at her. She braced herself for what he had to say.

"Well, Agent Ivanova, I'm glad to see you alive and in one piece. Also, I'd like to tell you, because of tonight's events you will not be held accountable for the last forty-eight hours. That means your file will stay unblemished and intact. But I warn you, don't try this again...otherwise, I won't be so forgiving. Understand?"

You're all heart, she thought, but decided not to voice that fact. She had almost died several times over the course of the night and so had Lucas. Mishkin thought she was worried about her record or her job at SVR?

She gave him a tired smile. *Don't burn your bridges, Elena*, she told herself.

"Perfectly, Director Mishkin. Thank you. Also, you may want to look into Yuri Volstov. I believe he's involved. Alexei mentioned the plot was a way to clear the path for Volstov to become president."

Mishkin nodded curtly to her before joining his superiors at the bomb sight. He wasn't really such a bad guy. Just one who was very rigid with his rules. Just as she had been prior to meeting Lucas. It was strange. Even in the years she'd been married to Nikolai, not once had she forgone the rigid guidelines which governed her life and career. Yet in just two days Lucas had irreparably changed her. She wondered what she would do once he was gone from her life.

The paramedic caught her attention. "Okay, we're going to take you to hospital now."

She shook her head then instantly regretted it as it began to pound steadily.

"You need to be under supervision. You have a concussion and need to be monitored," the medic continued.

"No, it's fine, really. I'll have my brother wake me every two hours okay? I just want to go somewhere I feel comfortable and rest up."

The medic nodded. "Fine, but if you feel any dizziness or nausea you come straight down to the hospital."

She confirmed she understood and got up slowly from the back of the ambulance, her body tired and aching. She watched the vehicle drive away before turning toward a fellow agent and asked for his phone. She quickly dialed Dmitry, who no matter what time of day or night seemed to be wide awake. She was concerned that he streamlined caffeine. But that was a worry for another time. She outlined her night and he told her to check into a hotel and he would see her soon. She did as he ordered. After collapsing into the nearest bed, Dmitry woke her two hours later when he arrived at her hotel. He hugged her tight, almost crushing her before asking how Lucas was doing. She burst into tears as her tightly held restraint disintegrated, her body long past exhaustion. Dmitry held her while she sobbed herself into oblivion.

Epilogue

One week later
Moscow Domodedovo Airport,
Russian Federation

The international departures lounge was bustling full of activity. Elena's heart ached as Lucas made his way back from the ticket office, his arm in a sling to restrict movement in his shoulder. She had been told he would have weeks of physical therapy to endure when he got home, the bullet having severed tendons and muscles that would need time to heal.

SVR had done a massive man-hunt, locating the agents among the agency who had sided with Alexei Dimitrovich against the president. They had turned up over twenty agents involved in selling information and providing insurance to a number of criminals. Director Mishkin had not been pleased with the turn of events and had vowed to have more vigorous in-house sweeps to weed out the undesirables.

Elena had gone back to her job as if nothing had happened. She was thankful for the mundane paperwork. Never again would she take it for granted, and planned on driving herself hard enough to forget the amount of times she had almost died, not to mention the two men in her life, Nikolai and Lucas. Her heart could take no more hits. She was barely holding on without going insane. She wondered if she'd ever stop feeling like this.

"I see you have your souvenir," she commented, trying to keep their conversation light. She swallowed in an attempt to dislodge the large lump in her throat and refrained from telling him she didn't want him to go. She had to protect her heart as much as she could and making it harder on the both of them certainly wouldn't help.

Her emotions were a jumble and her thoughts a mess. She felt as if she was being torn in two. Still in love with one man but feeling as if she were falling hard for another. As much as she didn't want him to go, she knew she couldn't promise him anything. It wasn't fair on him to even hint at a future. She was a mess right now and she needed time to heal. Her heart broke a little as she thought about this being the last time she'd ever see him.

Lucas looked down at the sling and grinned. "From Russia with love, right?"

Her heart rolled over. *Right, from Russia with love…my love*, Elena thought. So much for trying to protect her heart. She had successfully avoided that subject since the moment she'd met him, and now it was front and center in her mind. She wanted to weep. She gave him a smile she didn't feel and said,

"Well, Special Agent Gates, it was a real pleasure working with you."

***

Lucas nodded. "Thank you, and a pleasure working with you too, Agent Ivanova," he replied, keeping with her formal tone.

After everything they had gone through, this was it, a formal goodbye from the lounge of the airport? Where had he gone wrong? It was right after he fell in love with her.

He knew better than to fall for an attached woman.

He shook her hand, trying to ignore the feel of her soft skin and the sweet flowery smell of her perfume. He would never be rid of that scent. He would forever be haunted by the sweet smell of gardenias.

"So," he said, feeling numb. He'd never felt so desolate before. So desperate, as she slipped through his fingers. "You've come to see me off?"

"Actually, Director Mishkin wanted me to ensure that you got on the plane."

"Doesn't want me here anymore, huh?"

Elena nodded. "He said, and I quote, 'I'm sure America can't wait to have him back and we shouldn't deprive her of him.' So, yes, he can't wait to have you gone."

The public announcer came on and announced his flight was now boarding. He sent a look of regret to Elena.

"That's me."

She gave a small nod and he saw her eyes mist. Maybe she was sad to see him go after all? His heart did a happy dance in his chest. As much as Elena could be an open book, the past few days her face had been carved in stone, giving him little to work with. Certainly no hope for a possible future. He'd wondered if it had all been one-sided.

"Hey, what's this?" he asked as he wiped at a tear that rolled down her cheek.

"You're an amazing man, Lucas Gates, and I wish things were different," she said, her voice quivering.

"Don't cry, Elena. It might not be forever. I can wait for you. When you're ready, just let me know."

He leaned towards her, giving her time to back away. He could understand her situation. Until six months ago she was happily married. Then the love of her life was gone, murdered. Ripped abruptly from her. She hadn't fully dealt with that fact before she had developed feelings for him. And she did have feelings for him, of that he was now absolutely sure. She might not love him, not like he did her. But he was a patient man. He could wait forever if he had to. She was certainly worth it.

His lips skimmed lightly over hers, tasting her. Just a tease, then it was gone. He pulled back and stared into turbulent grey pools of emotion, as if she could no longer hold back her feelings any longer. She blinked a couple times before flinging herself against his body. He took a step back to accommodate the impact. She wrapped her arms tightly around his neck as she kissed him thoroughly, her tongue sliding over his when his lips parted. His arms snaked around her waist and held her tight against him. The entire airport melted away as he focused entirely on her and what she was doing to him.

He groaned and took control, kissing her deeply, devouring her as if her breath gave him life. The electricity that had always been between them ignited and zinged through his blood, snapping with its intensity. He felt it down to his toes and swore they curled as passion unfurled in his belly. It was an exquisite torture. A hunger consumed him deep within, leaving him breathless and aching. He felt himself begin to lose control and knew if he didn't stop now he never would. He set her aside and willed his body to stand down. When he glanced over at Elena, he was pleased to see her eyes were dark with desire. Her chest rose and fell with her deep breaths and he felt immense satisfaction that she was just as affected.

He knew there would never be another woman for him.

And why should he want one? He had everything he could ever want in this gorgeous package right in front of him. He cupped her cheek, feeling her exquisitely soft skin beneath his hand as he drank her in, drowning in those stormy grey eyes. She turned her head and placed a kiss on the palm of his hand.

"I promise, Elena," he said huskily before leaning in and pressing his lips once more to hers. A reminder of the future they could have.

He made himself step back from her before he did something stupid like throw her down and make love to her on the floor of the airport. He bent down and picked up his small travel bag.

He started walking away from her, but she stepped forward.

"Goodbye," she said, her voice filled with unshed tears.

He took her hand and squeezed, hoping his feelings were reflected in his eyes. He wanted no misunderstandings between them. He needed her to believe in him, in them. Nothing in his life had ever been more important.

"*Do svidaniya, moya lyubov.*" *Goodbye, my love.* He winked, dropped her hand, then turned and started towards the boarding gate before she could reply.

***

Eighteen Months Later,
Annandale, Virginia, USA

Lucas opened the external door to his kitchen. The feeling he was not alone washed over him in a flash from all his years of training. The air inside the room smelled different, carrying small scent particles from the intruder towards him. He removed his weapon from his belt holster and held it away from his body, ready to fire if or when needed. He controlled his breathing, bringing it to a steady inhale and exhale so he could listen for other noises as he silently moved toward the door separating the kitchen from the rest of the house.

A dark figure approached the doorway. The

outline of the body was male and tall. Lucas kept his gun trained and ready. His index finger barely touched the trigger but would not hesitate should he be required to shoot. His eyes remained on the man before him while his mind assessed the situation. The light from the moon outside spilled through the open-curtained window and streaked across the face of his intruder. His breath exhaled heavily as he recognized the man standing in his doorway. He switched on the light and watched as Dmitry Ivanov blinked at the sudden brightness, his eyes adjusting to the harsh glare.

"Jesus Christ, Dmitry," he scolded. "I could have damn near shot you."

Dmitry leaned a heavy hip against the entry-way into the kitchen. It was as if he no longer had the strength to keep standing. He let out a deep sigh, one that told Lucas that he had tried to think of other ways of dealing with his problem without having to involve the man who had almost become his sister's lover. "Sorry, Lucas, but I need your help."

"No shit," he replied sarcastically.

Acknowledgments

I'd like to thank the awesome staff at Limitless Publishing for helping me realize my dream and supporting me through each step, and to my editor Rosa. Each hand involved has made this book better. A big shout out to Dixie: I appreciate all your hard work and assistance. I'd also like to thank my friends who are always encouraging and supportive.

About the Author

Camille Taylor is an Australian author who resides in the Nation's Capital with her small dog. She was the typical 90's kid and was raised on Goosebumps, Roald Dahl and Paul Jennings. In her teens she began reading the Queen of Crime, Agatha Christie and in later years found Christine Feehan, Janet Evanovich and Julie Garwood.

She started writing at sixteen and enjoys spending time with her family, doting on her nieces and nephews, writing the many stories floating about her head and working on her genealogy where she can trace her heritage to England, Scotland, Ireland and Russia.

Her other interests include, anything creative—such as scrapbooking and drawing and has travelled across Western Europe, New Zealand and the UAE, after spending a year living in London. She's also dabbled in tae kwon do.

Facebook:
https://www.facebook.com/CamilleTaylorAuthor

Twitter:
https://twitter.com/CamilleTaylorAu

Website:
https://camilletaylorbooks.wordpress.com/

Goodreads:
https://www.goodreads.com/author/show/7791241.
Camille_Taylor